MW00943422

The *Jaws*
of the *Dragon*

The *Jaws* of the *Dragon*

Alan Gibbons

 Lerner Publications Company ■ Minneapolis

This edition first published 1994 by Lerner Publications Company, 241 First Avenue North, Minneapolis, Minnesota, 55401. For sale only in the United States and its territories.

Originally published in the United Kingdom by J.M. Dent & Sons Ltd.

Text copyright © 1991 Alan Gibbons

All rights reserved. International copyright secured. No part of this book may be reproduced or transmitted in any form or by any means, electronic or mechanical, including photocopying and recording, or by any information storage or retrieval system, without permission in writing from Lerner Publications Company, except for the inclusion of brief quotations in an acknowledged review.

Library of Congress Cataloging-in-Publication Data

Gibbons, Alan.
  The jaws of the dragon / Alan Gibbons.
    p. cm.
  Summary: Eleven-year-old Tra and his family face an uncertain future in Vietnam when his father defies the head of the village committee.
  ISBN 0-8225-0737-4
  [1. Vietnam—Fiction.   2. Family life—Fiction.]   I. Title.
PZ7.G33912Jaw   1994
[Fic]—dc20
                                                      93-47126
                                                         CIP
                                                          AC

Manufactured in the United States of America
1 2 3 4 5 6 — I/BP — 99 98 97 96 95 94

To my mother and father

Contents

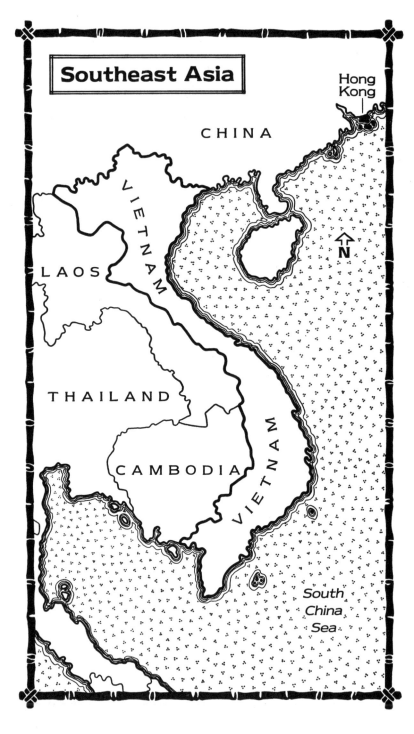

Southeast Asia

CHINA

Hong Kong

VIETNAM

LAOS

THAILAND

CAMBODIA

VIETNAM

N

South
China
Sea

Fighters

"Whenever I think of Vietnam I remember one late, thundery afternoon, years ago. It was during the summer months and the monsoon rains were falling. Not a soul ventured out onto the single dirt road through our hamlet, but under the drumming rain there was movement. Two dogs were fighting. The sound of their yelping and snarling drew me onto the porch of our house. I peered at the fighters through the leaves of a palm that swung heavy with the downpour. At first sight, it looked like an unequal battle. One of the animals was big and well fed for a village dog. It was astride its scrawny rival, lunging and biting. Its victim was squirming

9

uncontrollably on its back. As it snapped and snarled at its tormentor, I could see its ribs poking through its dull brown skin. Its big dark eyes stared up at the larger beast's powerful jaws, as they reached down and tore.

I yelled at the dogs, "Stop it! Stop!"

They took no notice. The big dog just reached down and tore again at the throat of its rival. I don't know how the fight began, but somehow, I knew that the larger dog had started it. There was to be no quick and easy finish to the combat. But then, in the eyes of the larger dog, I glimpsed fear. It wanted to end the fight it had begun, but it didn't have the strength. Each time it tried to break off the fight, the smaller dog would twist wildly on the ground and snap at its opponent. So it continued, there in the pouring rain, the ripping and tearing of two creatures driven wild by fury and pain.

I could see drops of blood from the animals' wounds mixing with the streams of rainwater that ran across the ground. Now the smaller dog had the larger one by the throat. It had set its jaws. All the efforts of an animal more than twice its size failed to shake the small dog loose. The big dog was whining, trying to pull away but failing at each attempt. It was desperate, but it was also weary. Its great head sagged. It began to writhe, wrenching its head from side to side, but the jaws of its scrawny rival did not relax. They couldn't relax; they clung on. All the strength of that small brown dog was in those jaws.

At last the big dog staggered. Its head hung like ripe fruit on a branch, ready to drop. It staggered again, then sank to the ground. Its flanks heaved for a moment or two, then it was still, lifeless. The victor rose unsteadily. It took a few slow steps, then passed out of my sight behind a bamboo hedge.

I slipped on my sandals and ran out, braving the rains. I found the little dog sprawled, as still and motionless as its defeated enemy. I rested my hand on its back as if I could restore it to life, but the ripped and bleeding body was quite dead. Its victory had lasted minutes; no more.

I buried the dogs in the bamboo grove. That was the year of the worst floods in 60 years. It was the year that rice became scarce. Grandmother used to tell me that Vietnam is a dragon, the second dragon of Asia after China, but I can't think of our country as a dragon. I remember it as that emaciated little dog that began to die at its moment of victory.

By the time I had finished burying the dogs, the rain had eased, and the sky was brightening. As soon as I walked back into the house, Grandmother was at the door.

"So there you are, Tra. I need you to find old Phao. He's wandered off again."

"Have you looked in his corral, Grandmother?" I asked. I knew she had, but I didn't want to wander the village looking for the old buffalo. After what I'd seen, I wanted to be left alone for a while to collect my thoughts—perhaps to rummage in my father's box of books. I wanted to fathom the mysteries of those crumpled, well-thumbed volumes. They fascinated me.

"Get going!" scolded Grandmother. "And don't spend too long finding him. I'm going to boil the rice."

Reluctantly I obeyed. The books would have to wait for another time. I could see my mother playing with Mai. We didn't look like brother and sister. Mai was a sturdy little thing who, even as a young child, had the look of a natural athlete. She took after my mother, with her dark, soft eyes and easy grace. I've always been my father's son, thin and angular. My little sister was giggling happily. I smiled, then turned toward the tree line that shielded the village. Phao was usually to be found out there on the edge of the rice fields. I pushed through hanging leaves, which were still laden with the afternoon rain, and looked across the rice paddies to our little river that led out toward the great Mekong.

A man was guiding his sampan out onto the water, now that the rain had stopped, but I couldn't make out who it was. He was dark against the gleaming water. I thought of the words of a song my mother sang:

> Come back to the village.
> A boat waits on the river.

I wanted my own boat, just like that man. I loved boats, especially since I had learned to row Hoan's sampan. Sometimes Hoan would laugh and call me "boat boy." I liked the sound of that—boat boy.

If I had a dream, it was to sail the oceans and read during the long, lazy days. The nearest I ever came to the sea was when my father went to work on the motor of a fishing vessel and took me with him. While he stripped it down, I lay on the deck and looked up at the sky, feeling the motion of the waves and the kiss of the breeze. Sometimes I thought that all I needed in life was to see the wind rushing across the water, and know that my family was near. Life was uncomplicated in those moments, and seemingly without hatred, or anger, or cruelty.

"Phao," I called. "Phao!"

I knew he would be somewhere close by. He didn't like to be shut up in that tiny corral by the house. Like the other village buffalo, he wandered in search of food. Unfortunately, unlike the other buffalo, Phao didn't know when to come home. I searched among the bushes and trees for his flat horns and strong, heavy shoulders, but there was no sign of him.

I was about to call Phao again, when I heard raised voices. One of them was familiar—it was my father's. I wondered what he was doing by the paddy fields. He had gone to the other end of the village that morning. Mother had said he was working on an irrigation pump. Our village, like many others in Vietnam, was a collection of tiny hamlets, strung out along a single rough track and crossed by a railway line. I edged toward the voices and crouched behind a palm.

I could see my father clearly, but the other man's face was hidden by the leaves. I recognized him the moment he spoke. It was Thuan, head of the village committee. He'd had this position of influence since the end of the American war. I didn't like him or his sharp-tongued son, Hung.

Thuan was talking about the irrigation pump. "I'm waiting for an explanation. How does a new pump break like that? I'll have to report this, you know."

There was anger in my father's voice as he replied, "New? Did you say new? Those parts were worn out before they were installed. You're not going to blame me for that. If new parts were sent, then they've found their way to the black market by now!"

I found it hard to make sense of the quarrel, but I did know that it was about more than just an irrigation pump.

Thuan's voice turned into a squeal of anger. "Take care what you're saying. In this village, I represent the government. If you're saying those parts were stolen, then that's a very serious allegation. In your position, I would try to control my tongue."

My father's eyes flashed. "What do you mean, my position?"

"I think you know," said Thuan.

"If you have something to say to me, be man enough to say it out loud. Tell me what you mean, Thuan." My father's voice sounded controlled, but there was a menace in his words I barely recognized.

"Our men have gone to fight the Cambodians, and behind Cambodia stands China, but you know that, don't you, Chinese brother?"

My blood ran cold at the way Thuan said "Chinese brother." I looked at my father's face. He looked shocked. His family were Hoa, people who had come south from China and settled in Vietnam's northern provinces, but why did that matter? There are over a million people of Chinese descent in Vietnam. Why did Thuan throw it in Father's face like that?

Thuan seized on my father's look of surprise. "You don't like me mentioning that, do you? Well, I know all about you people. We talked about it at the Party meeting. Don't think you can hide just because you married a Vietnamese. You're not from our village. We're watching you, Chinese brother."

My father was struggling to control his emotions. I saw his eyelids flickering, his usually impassive face betraying his shock and anger, but he recovered enough to protest. "I am as Vietnamese as you are, Thuan. You know that. I was born here...."

Thuan snorted. "Why do you protest so much? Have you got something to hide? Just remember what I said—we're watching you. Now, I want that pump repaired and no more talk about the black market. Throwing accusations about would be unwise in your position."

Just then I heard a throaty cough behind me. It was Phao, pushing his muzzle into my back. I hissed at him to be quiet but it was too late. The two men turned toward me.

Thuan walked away repeating his threat, "We're watching you."

Father frowned. "How much of that did you hear, Tra?" he asked.

I hesitated, then said, "I heard most of it. I heard him call you 'Chinese brother.' Why did he say that?"

"I don't know, but I think he dislikes me. He's a real troublemaker." Then, abruptly changing the subject, Father said, "Let's get Phao home."

As far as my father was concerned, our conversation was over. I picked up a bamboo switch and began to guide the old buffalo along the path toward our house.

Father limped behind me. He had an old injury that made walking painful. I glanced back at him and wondered what Thuan had been talking about. Why did it matter that Father wasn't from our village? I longed to question him, but he never talked about himself very much. It occurred to me that I barely knew my own father. His past was hidden. I knew the bare details, of course. My grandparents came from China and settled first in northern Vietnam before moving south to Saigon. I can't say that I thought much about my roots. I was a Vietnamese boy, growing up in the aftermath of a 10,000-day war. For some of the older people in our village, the war against the Americans—and the French before them—cast a long shadow over their lives. I didn't let it bother me, and I didn't really think about the fighting that had just broken out on the Cambodian border. I lived in a country where war always lurked in the wings. I hoped it would stay there.

When we got home, I coaxed Phao into his corral. Father leaned against the wall of our house beside my mother. She was swinging in the hammock while Mai ran back and forth. Mai was playing her favorite game. The moment anybody climbed into that hammock she would be there, trying to overturn the hammock and dump the person out.

Mother leaned out every time Mai ran past, trying to swat her. Mai squealed whenever Mother's hand reached toward her. Sometimes I envied Mai. She was six years old, five years younger than me, and everybody babied her. In most families the youngest child had to take care of the buffalo, but not Mai.

I scratched Phao's rough neck and thought of the quarrel I had witnessed.

"What was it all about, Phao?" I murmured. "What's going on?"

The old buffalo grunted and rubbed his head against the corral gate. He wasn't troubled by such questions.

Questions

A fter the meal, my father sat on the porch, reading. I recognized the book, a volume of poetry by To Huu, who was called "the voice of the Vietnamese revolution." I'd heard a lot about him; the village committee saw to that. The poems were full of ringing calls to arms. The village committee loved them and would have liked us to know them by heart. I preferred the classic tale of Vietnam, *The Tale of Khieu,* a story of war, rebellion, and love—although there was a lot in it I barely understood. I also liked the Western books in that box of Father's.

As I crept closer to him, Father laid the book face down on the floor and sighed. He gazed out across the bamboo grove.

"Do you like these poems?" I asked.

Father started at my voice, then smiled thinly. "Do you? I hear they're required reading these days. There were times when you could get yourself shot for reading such stuff."

I frowned, then replied, "I don't really know if I like them or not. I don't like having to read them."

"Shall I pick something to read?" asked Father.

I realized that he had evaded my question but I let it go. He chose a book called *Great Expectations*. He had bought it when the Americans were here. I don't remember the other men in the village reading much. They almost always seemed to be working.

Father was different because he didn't often work in the rice fields. He was somehow set apart from the others. He could put his hand to just about any sort of broken machinery, whether it was a pump, a generator, an old motorcycle, or a truck from the city. Usually it would be tools for the paddies, or a job for the village committee, but most of all I looked forward to the times when he let me row him down the river to work on the fishing fleet. On those days, I really was the boat boy I dreamed of being.

Sometimes I watched him as he worked steadily, methodically, with infinite patience. I once asked him why he loved machinery so much.

He said, "I know the rules machines work to. They're all the same, you see. All you have to do is follow the rules; each part in its place. I wish people were like that."

I didn't understand what he was getting at, so I just smiled.

That evening I listened to Father reading aloud in that quiet, almost musical voice of his. The family was gathered around him. Mother was winnowing the rice, tossing it repeatedly in a big, round sieve. She took care not to spill a single grain, because rice was precious that year. Mother *belonged*—just like Grandmother—because she was born here. They were the land and the land was them. The rhythm of their lives was set by the planting, and the growing and the harvesting of the rice.

But Father? I always associated him in my mind with books or with machines. He was aware of a world beyond the village. Although I loved the village, I also longed to see that world beyond. Father's box of books was a window to it.

I could hear Grandmother talking to Mai through the thin partition wall that divided the house. She was trying to persuade her to go to bed. Mai was at the age when she would use any excuse to avoid going to bed.

"Grandmother, why are the men fighting?"

"Which men?" asked Grandmother. "I haven't seen anyone fighting."

"The bo dai, the soldiers. I saw Thang. He walks with a stick."

"Thang was wounded last month in the fighting on the border," replied Grandmother. "He stood on a land mine. He must have been one of the first to be injured."

I could tell by her voice that Grandmother didn't want to talk about the fighting, but Mai wasn't easily put off. She chirruped, "But I thought the Americans were the wicked ones."

"They did terrible things to this country," said Grandmother. "They set Vietnamese against Vietnamese."

I listened to her reluctant explanation and wondered how much Mai understood. Grandmother didn't sound as if she was talking to a little girl. She sounded more like she was thinking out loud. As for me, I hated all the talk of war. Why couldn't the war just go away and leave us alone?

"But why, Grandmother, why are there so many bad people?"

"Many armies have come to our country, little one. When the foreigners come, then the people fight for their fatherland."

Grandmother usually managed to settle Mai. She joined us on the porch and stared disapprovingly at Mother. "Children these days, Ty! They're so disobedient! Even the girls...."

"Oh, Mother, Mai's a good child. She's just

testing you, that's all."

Grandmother shook her head and began clearing the table.

I stole a glance at Father and then asked, "Why didn't you mention the Chinese, Grandmother?"

Father stopped reading. I continued quickly, "You didn't tell Mai about the Chinese. Before the French or the Americans, we fought the Chinese. For centuries we fought them."

Grandmother glanced toward Father. "What makes you talk about these things, Tra?" she asked.

I glanced out at the bamboo as it dipped and swayed in the evening breeze. I could feel everyone's eyes upon me. I explained about Father's argument with Thuan.

"You shouldn't listen to men like Thuan," said Mother. "He wants to be a big, important man. He would walk on the bodies of other men to get what he wants."

"But is he right? Are the Chinese behind the Cambodians?"

"Perhaps he is right about that. Things are bad between China and Vietnam. China will use anyone to make trouble for Vietnam. This time it's the Cambodians."

"But what does that mean for us?" I asked. "What are we? You can't have two countries, can you?"

Father rose stiffly and walked away without a word.

Mother looked after him. "Your father's family once came from China," she said. "But he loves Vietnam. He was born here. It's his country—and yours too—despite men like Thuan."

Mother tried to return to the rice, but I wasn't finished yet. "Father wasn't here very often when I was little, was he?"

Mother smiled and said, "Do you remember that, the times he was away?"

I nodded and added, "I think I remember him coming sometimes in the night and holding me. I think so."

Mother said, "I didn't dream you would remember those times, Tra. You were very young, not much more than a baby."

But I wasn't a baby anymore. A lot had happened since then and now I had to answer for what I did, and for what I was. As I watched my father walking slowly down the road, two sounds filled my mind. One was Phao's throaty grumbling in the corral. The other was the memory of Thuan's words—Chinese brother, Chinese brother.

Thang

In the days that followed, I don't remember hearing anyone talk about Chinese brothers. There had never been any hostility between the Vietnamese and the Chinese in our district. Most of the Chinese ran shops in the town, our provincial capital. The people in our village didn't even talk about the Vietnamese or the Chinese. They just talked about the floods, the price of rice, and—when Thuan wasn't around—the interference of the village committee. Everyone resented it. We might have a village committee to act as the eyes and ears of the new government, but governments and committees don't harvest rice. Thuan certainly didn't. He just swanked around with Hung tagging along behind him.

Grandmother was grumbling. "Do you know what I heard in the market? There are people eating sorghum because there isn't enough rice. Sorghum! That's animal feed!"

Father reacted strangely to her complaining. Sometimes he would mutter, "Does she expect us to recover from 30 years of war overnight?"

More often he would look away and ignore Grandmother's grumbling. I couldn't understand his attitude. It was as if he felt responsible for the food shortages, but that was crazy. Wasn't it the 30 years of war that were to blame, and maybe crooks like Thuan who seemed to be manipulating things to suit themselves?

One afternoon, the whole village was working in the rice fields to transplant the rice. The men, women, and older children were stooping in the muddy paddies, pulling up clumps of rice stalks. The younger children were dancing along the ditches and dikes, playing and laughing like flocks of birds. My father, as usual, was at the edge of things, trying to mend an old irrigation wheel. The villagers had long since given up on the irrigation pumps that had been sent from the city. Either they broke down, or the gasoline to drive them didn't arrive on time. I had expected my father to be in trouble with Thuan over that, but I needn't have worried. Everyone just shrugged their shoulders and got on with things. Nobody had expected the pumps to work.

Duong and his sister, Lanh, were working on either side of me by the dike. They were my best friends.

Pausing as he tugged at the rice stalks, Duong said, "Did you hear what Hung has been saying about you?"

I shook my head, but I knew what was coming next.

"He says your father is on the side of the Cambodians. Hung says your father celebrated when they shelled our villages."

Lanh stared at her brother. "Why are you telling him that? Hung is stupid. He just repeats what he hears. Let's talk about something else."

I didn't want to talk about something else, but I didn't know how to argue with what Hung had said, so I just asked, "When did he say that?"

Duong leaned forward, excited at the prospect of a fight between Hung and me. He was so dense sometimes. He opened that big mouth of his before considering the damage he might do. He just didn't think.

"He never stops repeating it," Duong continued. "He really has it in for you and your father. Do you know why?"

I looked away.

"He says you Chinese have been our enemies for centuries."

"Duong!" exclaimed Lanh. "I think you've said enough."

I had certainly heard enough. Duong might relish a fight, but I was always one to walk away from trouble. I rose and made my way along the dike to where my father was working. It was all his fault. It was Father who was Chinese, not me. Why should I have to answer for him? Father scratched his nose, glanced at me for a moment, then resumed his work.

Duong and Lanh caught up with me and gave me a shove. We raced along the dike, overtaking Thang, a young soldier back from Cambodia. Jostling for position, Duong tried to pass, but he lost his footing and slithered into the muddy water of the paddy.

Lanh laughed and said, "That will teach you, you idiot!"

Grinning broadly, Duong began to clamber up the dike. Suddenly the smile vanished from his face.

I was about to ask him what the matter was, when I heard a terrible cry.

It was Thang. He had fallen and was lying on the ground, twisting and writhing in agony. His crutches lay beside him, and his face was drawn with pain as he clutched at the stump of what had been his leg. It had recently been amputated at the knee. The loose-hanging trouser leg was soaked in fresh blood.

We ran to him. "What's wrong, Thang? What's wrong?" I asked stupidly.

"Can't you see? It's his leg," snapped Duong.

"Stay with him," I gasped. "I'll get my father."

I raced across the dike, scrambling to keep my footing on the slippery earth. I was frightened.

"Father, Father! Come quickly! It's Thang. He's collapsed and his leg's bleeding. He looks so strange...."

"Thang? Where is he?"

I led the way. Father pushed forward to examine him. I wasn't looking at the soldier, I was staring at Father. He ripped open the trouser leg and inspected Thang's stump.

I heard him draw in his breath sharply.

"What is it?" I asked.

"The leg. It's infected. If we don't get him to a hospital, he could die."

"Die, did you say?" It was Hoan, Duong and Lanh's father. "We have to do something fast."

Hoan's voice was drowned by the roar of an engine. A battered old army truck lurched into view down the road through the forest and stopped at the edge of the paddy.

"You're right," said Father. "We have to do something and I know what." He walked quickly but awkwardly, swinging his bad leg as he approached the truck.

I could see Thuan and Hung sitting in the cab. Thuan was peering through the window in the direction of Thang.

"What's going on?" he demanded.

"It's Thang. His leg has become infected where they amputated. The conditions in some of those battlefield hospitals are dreadful. It's butchery, not surgery."

"What makes you such an expert?" Thuan asked coldly, as he changed gears.

"I've got some medical training," explained Father. "Now look, I need your truck. We've got to get him to the provincial hospital."

Thuan's eyes flashed. "You *need!* Since when do you give orders? If he has to go to the hospital, then I'll take him."

Father looked angry. He stepped onto the running board and tugged at the door handle.

"Don't you understand? The boy could die. I know you don't like me much, Thuan, but you're not a medical man. I'm the best qualified to help him."

Thuan hesitated. Attracted by Thang's cries and the sound of raised voices, a few villagers had gathered around the truck.

"Let him have the truck," said Hoan. "If we can send boys like Thang to war, then we should look after them when they come home all busted up."

There was a murmur of agreement from the small crowd. It was all the encouragement that Father needed. He wrenched open the door and leaned into the cab. "Well, do I get the truck?"

Thuan scowled, then got out, followed by Hung. While the villagers made Thang as comfortable as possible in the back, Thuan glared at Father. He was furious. I knew the incident was bound to lead to trouble, but I didn't care. Just then, I couldn't have felt any prouder.

"Tra," came Father's voice. "Get in. I'll need somebody to help me with Thang. Hoan, can you let Thang's family know? Call on Ty as well."

Hoan nodded. As the truck pulled away, I waved to Duong and Lanh.

The Town

"You're not from around here, are you, boy?"
The speaker was an old man sitting in a sampan. I stared at him, then at the bustling traffic and the street vendors with their pots of boiling noodles, their watches, and their cheap trinkets. I certainly wasn't from around here. To me, the town seemed very strange. Everybody was selling something or hurrying somewhere. There didn't seem to be any place where you could just sit still and be by yourself.

"No," I answered. "We brought a sick man to the hospital. There's no doctor in our village."

"We?" asked the old man, looking around. "I don't see anyone else."

"My father is with Thang in the hospital. He lost part of his leg in Cambodia, and the stump isn't healing properly."

The old man shook his head, which made his wispy white beard wave like the hair on a buffalo's tail. "Wars are bad things. I was hurt in the war, you know. Look here."

He raised a thin but muscular arm. There was a scar running from his elbow to his shoulder. "An American soldier did that. He came up and said, 'You Viet Cong?' When I didn't answer, he gave me a jab with his bayonet—"

The old man stopped midsentence and asked, "What's up? What are you frowning at, boy?"

"You said Viet Cong," I replied. "What's that?"

"That's what the Americans and their allies called the National Liberation Front. Surely you've heard of them."

"Of course I have," I said. "I just hadn't heard the resistance called Viet Cong. Were you NLF?"

"Me?" The old man laughed. "Just ask anyone around here about old Ro. Do you know what they'll say? 'Him, he's out for himself.' They'd be right, too. You don't catch me fighting for anyone, not the Americans, not the Communists."

I looked at the sampan bobbing among a flotilla of small boats.

"Do you want to take a look?"

I nodded and clambered aboard.

"Is this how you make a living?" I asked, glad for a chance to take my mind off Thang. That's why I had left Father at the hospital. Instinct had brought me down to the river.

"That's right. I transport things."

"Like what?"

"Anything I can sell at a profit." Ro leaned forward and gave a mischievous grin. "Promise you won't tell the authorities."

I smiled. It was pleasant sitting here in the shadow of the bridge and being rocked by the lazy motion of the river. There was a loud, steady hiss made by the hundreds of bicycles passing overhead. Occasionally a truck rumbled by.

"Of course, you need a bigger boat than this to earn real money," said Ro.

"What do you mean?"

"Don't tell me you don't know that either? They're leaving in the thousands, from all over Vietnam."

"Who are?"

"The ones who want to get out, of course— the boat people. South Vietnamese army types, and the Chinese, of course. Anybody who can pay for their passage."

"But where are they going?"

"Anywhere that will have them—America, Canada, Australia. You know what one guy said to me just last week? 'I'll give you 200,000 dong if you can find me a boat.'"

Ro leaned forward and pointed upriver. "He'll be out there by now on the South China Sea. Good luck to him, I say. Good luck to anybody who pays me 200,000 dong for a nod in the right direction. The more the merrier."

Another voice broke in on the conversation. A younger man in a green, army-surplus helmet was scowling. "You talk too much, Ro. You'll have the security police down on us."

Ro just grinned. He jerked his thumb at a flag flying above an official building, a gold star on a red background, the flag of the new Vietnam.

"Why should they do anything to the likes of me? I'm just getting rid of a problem for them. A million Chinese too many? Just stick them on a boat and wave them good-bye. Besides, have you ever seen an official who wouldn't turn a blind eye for a few dong? Like they say, money talks."

I felt the back of my neck bristling at the mention of the Chinese. "I have to be going now. My father will be worried."

I stumbled off the sampan onto the bank and climbed back to the main road. Ro stared after me, puzzled by my sudden departure. I hurried back along the acacia-lined avenue that led to the hospital. The stay in town had been like an adventure until then. I hadn't even minded sleeping in the back of the truck the night before.

The busy, bustling streets were beautiful in

their own way, bordered by gardens of mimosa and jasmine and banks of red and purple bougainvillaea. There was beauty too in the old French villas, some of them still bullet-pocked from the war. Yet behind the beauty, something was wrong. How could Ro be doing so well from the misfortune of others?

Father called to me from the front of the hospital. "Tra, there you are. Good news. We can go home. Thang's mother and brother are here. They'll stay with him now. Our job is done."

"How is he?"

"Thang? He'll mend. He's young and strong. He would have died if he hadn't had medical attention though. They're short of medical supplies here, but at least they've got antibiotics and sterile dressings."

I climbed into the truck.

As we pulled out slowly into the stream of cyclists passing over the bridge, I looked down at the bobbing sampans.

Tonight, I thought, somebody else will be handing over a wad of money to get a passage out of here.

Father noticed me staring at the boats. "I can guess where you've been—hanging around the boats as usual."

I stared out of the window.

"Is something wrong? You're not sick, are you?"

"I met a man called Ro. He says all the Chinese are leaving. They're paying to get out on boats."

Father overtook a pedicab driver and glanced at me. "He's right, they are leaving. They're sick of being abused. There are people running this country who want to blame the Chinese for everything that's going wrong."

"But that can't be true...." I started to interrupt.

"Of course it's not true," Father sighed wearily. "It was American bombs that fell from the skies, wasn't it? It's American politicians now who refuse aid to a half-starved country. Why blame Chinese people who just want to make a living? We're just scapegoats."

Father was grim-faced now. He was glad to have me with him, but my mention of the refugee trade had infuriated him. Sitting next to him, I could feel his bitterness. We drove on in silence. Soon, we were back in the countryside, where everything looked familiar.

The villagers stood ankle-deep in the muddy water of the paddies that stretched toward the hazy blue mountains in the distance. From time to time, the jungle covered the land like a vast carpet in varying shades of green. I had known this landscape all my life, and I should have been glad to be back. But I had been fascinated by the town, despite everything that was strange and threatening there.

Suddenly, without warning, Father stopped the truck and turned to me. "I didn't mean to snap at you, Tra. I'm sorry. I feel so angry. I got a letter from your uncle Duc the other day. A friend of his has just disappeared. It turns out the authorities towed his family out to sea in an old fishing boat. That's right, they threw him out of his country and abandoned him to the open sea. The man has lived here for 40 years. Where's the justice in that? The Chinese aren't leaving—they're being driven out."

"You hate the government, don't you?" I asked.

Father paused, weighing his words carefully. "I am angry at what Vietnam has become. A whole community is being persecuted, and that's not all. They say that there are thousands of people in re-education camps in the jungle. Nobody knows exactly how many. They're not all people who fought on the American side, either. People are being locked up for being intellectuals—teachers, lawyers, doctors, even musicians. Locked up without even a trial. It's madness. And while they lock up the intellectuals, people like Thuan get fat on the black market."

Restarting the engine, Father reached over and rested his hand on my arm for a second. It was unlike him. I looked out of the window and watched the endless rice fields flashing past, and all the time I thought of his anger and bitterness....

"Tra, wake up. We're home."

I rubbed my eyes. "How long have I been asleep?" I asked, surprised.

"Over an hour. Uh oh! What's this? It looks like we've got a reception committee."

On the road in front of us stood Thuan and two other members of the village committee. Father sighed and muttered, "Stay here. This can only mean trouble."

I waited in the cab, but I could hear Thuan's words clearly. I dug my fingernails into my palms.

"You've gone too far this time, Loc. This is a serious matter, taking state property by force and insulting a district official. You're being summoned to a meeting of the village committee. You've got two days to prepare a defense. I advise you to think seriously about what you are going to say."

Di Chui

▼

"What can they do to you, Father?"
"I don't know. These village committees have only been around since the Americans
left. You never know, it might be all talk. It
usually is with men like Thuan."

I wasn't so sure. I remembered the look on
Thuan's face when Father had thrown him out
of the truck in front of everyone. It was the look
of hatred.

"This won't help, though," Father continued,
pulling a newspaper out of his pocket and handing it to me.

"What does it say?"

"Read it. If there's one thing I've done for you

in my life, it's to make sure you could read."

That was true. Father set aside part of every evening to read to Mai and me, and then he got us to read. I can even read English because of those evenings on the porch. I ran my eyes over the front page.

"The Chinese have invaded!" I gasped.

It was all there. Chinese divisions had poured across the border and partially destroyed the northern town of Lang Son.

"It's like a gift to Thuan. His kind have been trying to whip up hostility for months. Well, it won't be a whispering campaign now. He'll be out to destroy us."

When we reached the house, Mai was playing with a friend on the porch. The moment she saw Father, she began to squeal, "Daddy's back! Daddy and Tra are back!"

Grandmother was the first to appear, and she looked angry. "You've done it this time, Loc. Why can't you just keep your head down like other men? Why do you have to provoke them?"

"What do you mean, Sang?" demanded Father indignantly.

"Surely you know. The village committee has been round looking for you. That scoundrel Thuan was spitting fire about Chinese spies and fifth columnists. That's right, they think you're working among us for the enemy."

"I'm no spy and I'm no fifth columnist," Father

said quietly. "Where's Ty?"

"I know you're no spy," snapped Grandmother, ignoring Father's inquiry about Mother. "You don't need to be. As far as they're concerned, you're Chinese and that's all they need to know. It makes you guilty of anything they fancy. Why couldn't you keep quiet? Why didn't you let someone else take Thang to hospital?"

"And what if nobody else would?" asked Father. "What if they were all too frightened? What if I was the only one with the medical knowledge to take care of him? What should I do—let him die?"

Mother emerged from the house. Her eyes were red and I could tell that she'd been crying. She hissed, "Come into the house, the two of you. If somebody hears you and tells Thuan, it'll just make things worse."

I started to follow them into the house, but Grandmother wagged her finger at me and asked, "Where do you think you're going, Tra? This isn't for children to hear."

"What's wrong?" asked Mai as I sat down on the porch.

"You wouldn't understand," I snapped.

"I would understand," said Mai. "I would, so there."

I was in no mood to argue. I could see Duong and Lanh pushing their father's sampan out onto one of the little waterways alongside the paddies.

Suddenly, as I stood up, I felt a sharp pain in my calf. I spun around to see Mai racing back to the porch.

"You kicked me!" I yelled.

"You deserved it," shouted Mai. Her friend giggled.

I shook my fist at her, then laughed. It's hard to stay angry with her for very long. I set off to join Duong and Lanh.

"I'm surprised you came back," said Duong.

"I don't think I should have bothered," I sighed. "You've heard, I suppose, about Father?"

"It's all around the village," said Lanh. "Hung's been boasting about how his father's going to deal with our Chinese problem."

"He would," I observed, climbing into the sampan.

The moment I set foot on the boat, Duong started to rock it and nearly pitched me into the water. I recovered quickly and joined in the game. One of us was in for a soaking.

"Oh, not this game again!" complained Lanh, clinging to the sides of the sampan. "Why do you bother, Duong? Tra's bound to win."

"Not this time," shouted Duong. "Move over, Tra. I'm the new king of the boats...."

Before Duong could finish, I caught him off balance by putting all my weight on one side of the sampan. Landing in a heap on the matting that covered the floor of the sampan, he accepted defeat.

"OK, you win again, boat boy. You can row."

"Where?"

"I don't know. Over there."

Duong pointed to a small group of villagers transplanting rice. One of them was singing:

"I see a boat on the river, it's sailing away
Down to the ocean, where to I can't say."

"Everybody's singing that just lately," said Duong sarcastically.

"No wonder," sighed Lanh. "All those boat people. The Nguyen family left last week. Two families have gone from just up the river. Father says it's getting to be the same in every village."

"The Nguyens aren't Chinese," I observed.

"You don't have to be," said Duong. "Loads of people are going. You know Kim in our class?"

I nodded.

"Well, his uncle left on an old fishing boat, but he got caught by the security police. He'd only been at sea for half an hour. He says he's going to try again though."

Lanh leaned forward as if to confide a secret. "Father says he'd go tomorrow if he could get on a boat."

I was shocked. "Surely you don't mean it?" I said.

"Why not? Things are getting worse. The

shortages, the taxes, being told what to grow."

"You sound just like your father," I said.

"I can think for myself, you know." Lanh scowled.

"Sorry," I said. "I didn't mean to be rude."

"Go on," urged Duong. "Be rude. You have my permission."

"You'd better be careful, little brother," warned Lanh. "I can still beat you up."

"She can, too," said Duong with a grin.

The sampan slid past a group of women walking along the water's edge. We heard their whispered words—*"Di chui"*—escape.

"It's just like I said," announced Duong. "They all want to leave."

The Meeting

"Just watch yourself, Loc. Don't go sticking your neck out. Shooting your mouth off got you into trouble in the first place. It's time you remembered that you've got a family. Do you hear me, Loc? Your family must come first."

Father listened to Grandmother in silence. He sat on the porch, watching her through half-closed eyes, almost like a child sulking. I knew just how he felt. Nobody enjoyed Grandmother's scolding. Sometimes I think that she is the real head of our family.

"You'd better be going," said Mother anxiously. "It's almost time."

That afternoon my mother was as quiet as

Grandmother was irritable. They each had their own way of disguising the fear that had been growing for the past two days. I had never felt like this before. I'd been afraid of things like the dark, or thunder, or Hung's bullying, but I always got over that sort of fear. Mother, Father, and Grandmother were always able to reassure me. Now they seemed as powerless and nervous as I was.

I overheard them say that Father was being described as a "halfway element." I couldn't make much sense of it. I think it meant he was in trouble, but not deep enough to be locked up for it. I tried to ask my mother and grandmother about it, but they just changed the subject.

Father rose and took a step onto the dusty road. Mai raced over to him and threw her arms around him, burying her face in his shirt. Even my little sister knew there was a lot at stake.

"Hey now," said Father, tousling Mai's sleek black hair. "What's this? I'm only going to a meeting, you know. I'll be back for the evening meal." Slipping Mai's hands from his waist, Father set off.

"I'm worried, I don't mind telling you," said Grandmother.

Mother frowned and nodded furtively in the direction of Mai and myself. I let them think I hadn't heard. It always amazes me how obvious adults are about everything, even when they're trying to keep something secret. They're laughable, really, these attempts to "keep it from the children."

"I'm going over to see Lanh and Duong," I said.

"Okay," said Mother, "but don't be late getting back."

I found Duong down by the train crossing, lazily tossing stones at the warning light that hung over the track.

"They'll catch you one of these days," I called.

"Catch me?" asked Duong. "Catch me doing what?"

"You know very well—throwing stones at the trains, that's what! I've seen you do it. You could hurt someone."

Duong shrugged his shoulders and changed the subject. "When's your father got to go before the village committee?"

"He's there now."

"Are you scared?" asked Duong.

"Of course I am. Thuan's really got it in for him. I hate that man."

"You'd better keep that to yourself," said Duong. "He's the big cheese around here."

"Well, he shouldn't be. Grandmother says we fought the Americans to win our freedom. What sort of freedom is it when someone like Thuan can go around bullying everybody?"

"Beats me," said Duong, with a shrug of his shoulders. Then he asked, "Where's this meeting, anyway?"

"The village hall."

"I know," said Duong. "Why don't we go down there?" The meeting hall was about a 15-minute walk.

"We can't do that," I protested.

"Why not?" asked Duong. "If it were my father, nothing would keep me away."

The last gibe cut me to the quick. "All right, we'll go, but we've got to be careful. What if we get caught?"

Duong threw me a contemptuous look, and we set off. There was woodland all round one side of the village hall, and we were able to creep right up to it without being seen. Suddenly Duong began to climb a coconut palm overlooking the hall. I still wasn't sure about eavesdropping on the meeting, and I was terrified of being seen and making things worse for my father.

"Are you coming up or not?" hissed Duong.

I stared up at him. From where he was, he could have touched the tiled roof of the building. There was an open window hardly an arm's length from the branch on which he was sitting. I heard voices and ducked out of sight. It was the members of the village committee. Thuan was talking quickly and waving his arms. He was obviously already trying to win them over. How I hated him.

I heard a single word that filled me with dread: *reactionary*. Though I could only guess at its meaning, I knew from experience that anyone called a reactionary was in deep trouble.

The moment the door had closed behind the members of the village committee, Duong beckoned me to climb up next to him. Reluctantly I obeyed. I've never been very strong or agile, and by the time I had completed the climb, the hearing had begun. As I edged along the branch next to Duong, I was able to see the committee members at the front table and my father sitting alone on a chair in the middle of the hall, facing them.

"Your father just sat down," whispered Duong. "He told them what happened in the rice fields."

Thuan began to speak. "Comrade Hei, I can't accept the account Comrade Loc has given this committee." He spat out "Comrade Loc" as if he were cursing.

I glanced at the middle-aged woman to whom Thuan was addressing his remarks. Miss Hei, who was chairing the meeting, was our schoolteacher.

"You have the floor, Comrade Thuan," she announced.

"Let me begin with a question," said Thuan. "Isn't it true that I offered to take Thang to the hospital myself?"

"It is," replied Father. "But that's not the point...."

"Is your answer yes or no?" demanded Thuan.

"Look, it isn't that simple," Father protested.

"Yes or no?" demanded Thuan again.

I craned forward to hear Father's reply, but I must have ventured too far. Thuan cut short his interrogation and glanced up at the window.

"What is it, Comrade Thuan?" asked Miss Hei.

"I saw somebody spying on us," explained Thuan.

"We'd better take a look," said Miss Hei.

I heard the scrape of sandals on the floor of the hall.

"Now we're in for it," said Duong. "Get down—fast!"

I couldn't move. I was paralyzed, not so much by concern for myself, but because it might make things worse for Father.

"For goodness sake, Tra, move, will you?"

I realized that I had to escape and began to scramble down the trunk of the palm tree. Duong was shinning down after me.

"They're coming," he groaned. Even he was frightened now.

The door swung open.

"Jump!" urged Duong. "You've got to jump."

I did as he said, but I fell heavily. I tried to get up, but I stumbled and fell over again, finding myself at Thuan's feet as he emerged from the hall.

"What's your son doing here, Comrade Loc?" demanded Miss Hei as she glared at me from the doorway.

"I don't know," replied Father. "Are you all right, Tra?"

I nodded ruefully and picked myself up.

"Now go home," he ordered. His eyes were dark with anger. "I won't have you eavesdropping. Go on, and don't let me catch you here again."

My heart sank at the way he looked at me. I had betrayed him. As the door closed and the hearing began again, Duong dropped down beside me.

"Let's get out of here," he said.

I followed him miserably for a few minutes, and then snapped, "Why did I ever listen to you?"

"Don't blame me!" Duong yelled angrily. "You're the idiot who got us caught."

"I'm sorry," I murmured. "I'm angry with myself, not you."

Late that evening, we were still waiting for Father to return. Duong had hung around for an hour or two, but he gave up and went home when it got dark. Mother was keeping herself busy to hide her anxiety. Grandmother was having her usual struggle getting Mai to bed.

"I want to stay up until Father gets back," she wailed. "It's not fair. Why do I have to go to bed before Tra?"

"Tra is older. Now lie down and no more nonsense."

Grandmother kissed Mai and stepped onto the porch. We gazed together down the dusty road and on past the palm-shaded houses and the open-front shops. Dusk was gathering and a haze trembled over the rickety bamboo bridge Father had to cross on his way home.

Grandmother gave me a sidelong glance and said, "I just hope you didn't make things worse for Loc. Why did you do it, Tra? You knew how important that meeting was."

"Don't scold the boy, Grandmother," murmured Mother softly. "He just wanted to be with his father. You can't blame him for that."

"I suppose not," admitted Grandmother. "But where is Loc?"

Suddenly we heard footsteps behind the house. All of us stood up, but nobody dared to look. We waited nervously.

"Loc!" exclaimed Mother as he walked into view. "What do you think you're doing sneaking up on us like that? We didn't know who it was. We expected you to come from the opposite direction."

"I've been round at Thang's house," said Father, sitting down with his back against the wall.

"Thang? You mean he's back?"

"Yes, he's back, luckily for me."

"What do you mean?" asked Mother.

"The hospital released him. They needed the bed, and his leg was healing well. When he got home, he heard about the meeting and came to speak up for me. He's got guts, that young man. He hasn't done himself any favors by taking my part."

"Surely he owed it to you?" said Grandmother.

"That may be, but he could have kept quiet."

"So what happened?" demanded Mother.

"Thuan was swinging the committee over to his way of thinking. He wanted my head on a platter. He would have got it, too, but for young Thang. You should have seen Thuan's face."

"Tra nearly did," said Mother with a smile.

I lowered my eyes, but when I stole a look at Father he too was smiling. "Comrade Hei just stood up and closed the meeting. She gave Thuan such a withering stare."

"Does that mean we're safe?" asked Grandmother.

The smile vanished from Father's face. "I suppose it does...for now."

I examined Father's dark, troubled eyes and knew he was thinking of Thuan.

The Tunnel

Hoan let us have the sampan the next afternoon, and we made full use of his offer. Going farther afield than usual, we glided past grazing water buffalo with egrets perched on their broad backs. A heron soared over the paddies.

"Where do you want to go?" I asked.

"Anywhere," said Lanh.

"Let's take a look at the tank," suggested Duong. He'd always been fascinated by the rusty hulk of a North Vietnamese army tank that lay abandoned at the edge of the forest.

I looked at Lanh for approval.

"Why not?" she said, trailing her fingers lazily in the still water.

We moored the boat among tall, waving reeds and walked through the grass toward the canopy of trees ahead of us. Here and there, one tree towered high above the rest.

We soon found the tank.

Duong climbed onto the gun turret. "Imagine driving one of these," he shouted.

Lanh shuddered and said, "Imagine being trapped in one."

"There was a real battle out here," I said, running my hand over the rusting armor. "Just look at the wreckage."

"The fighting must have been part of the drive on Saigon," said Lanh. "Just before the final victory."

Suddenly Duong jumped down, urging us to take a look in the forest.

"Not over there," cried Lanh. "We're not supposed to go there. People have got terrible blisters on their feet after walking in there."

"I know, I know," said Duong. "I've heard it all before. 'Don't go there, don't go there.' We've just got to be careful."

I didn't think it was even possible to be careful in there. During the war, the Americans used lots of poisonous chemicals on the forest to kill the trees and undergrowth. It's said that for every man, woman, and child in Vietnam, they dropped more than six and a half pounds. They wanted to clear it and stop the NLF soldiers who were hiding there. Now the soil is poisoned, and the poison infects the water, the plants, even the people. In the hospital, Father had pointed out a room to me. He said it should be shown to everybody before they decide to go to war. The room contained the preserved bodies of stillborn children who had been damaged by the effects of chemicals.

Duong wasn't in the mood to listen to his sister. He plunged into the forest, calling back to us, "Do what you want. I'm going."

"Duong!" called Lanh, but he had disappeared behind the trees.

"Oh, why does he have to be so stubborn!" Lanh groaned.

We followed Duong into the forest. Just beyond the tree line stretched a tract of brownish scrub where chemicals had been dropped. The trees were bare and withered, and the only new growth was a tough, feathery wild grass. It was eerie the way stretches of earth were almost completely bare, while a short walk away the jungle grew as thickly as ever. Here a tree grew tall, orchids flourishing in its shade; there, just a hundred yards away, the trees were petrified. Not a leaf had grown for years.

"Duong!" Lanh yelled. "Where are you?"

We searched among the bushes and the lianas, which clung to the tree trunks.

"Did you see where he went?" Lanh asked anxiously.

"No. I don't understand it. He can't have gone far."

That's when Duong gave me the biggest shock of my life. I heard a pounding sound and felt movement under my feet. I jumped back.

Duong's head popped up out of the ground as he flung back a concealed door. He was grinning broadly.

"Isn't it great? It's one of the old tunnels."

Lanh was furious. "Are you crazy? Come out of there. It's really dangerous."

Duong ignored her and vanished back into the tunnel.

"Duong! You come out this minute!"

Duong's head popped out again. "I wish we had a lamp or something. I wonder how far the tunnels go."

"They run right under this part of the forest," I said. "Don't you remember that film we saw in school? They've shown it to us often enough."

"Tra's right," pleaded Lanh. "These tunnels stretch for many miles. You could get completely lost. You could die down there."

Duong hoisted himself up out of the hole. "Don't worry," he said. "Even I wouldn't go down there without a flashlight. I'd love to explore, though, wouldn't you, Tra?"

I decided it was best to keep quiet. That way, Lanh would think I was on her side and Duong would think I was on his.

"How long do you think people stayed down there?" Duong asked, peering into the darkness below the ground.

"In some parts of North Vietnam, whole villages had to live underground for days on end because of the bombing," said Lanh.

"Days!" exclaimed Duong. "Wouldn't that be great?"

"You wouldn't think so if you had to do it," snapped Lanh impatiently. "Kids always think things are exciting at first. You'd soon be bored."

"Who do you think you're calling a kid?" cried Duong. "You're only 13 yourself."

On the way back to the boat, Duong whispered, "The first time Lanh isn't with us, we'll come back."

I wasn't at all sure I wanted to go back, but I nodded.

Lessons

◆

It was hot inside the schoolroom. Next to me, Duong gazed longingly out at the motionless trees. He hated listening to anyone—especially Comrade Duy from the Youth League. Duy was speaking about Vietnam's centuries of struggle against the Chinese oppressors. At any other time I would have listened willingly to the old stories of resistance and heroism. I've heard them all from my mother and grandmother. Suddenly, though, the nation's history had become a weapon to be wielded against Vietnam's own Chinese population. We, and not China's mighty emperors, had become the enemy.

As I listened to the beautiful old stories of

national resistance, I began to loathe the boy standing in front of us. His talk was full of references to "Chinese domination" and "colonial tyrants." Why didn't he say what he meant? This wasn't history, it was hatred.

From time to time, Hung and his cronies turned and looked at me from their position in the front row. Hung was relishing every moment of the talk, every insinuation against the Chinese. He wanted revenge for his father's humiliation. I hoped against hope that there wouldn't be discussion after the talk. If there was, I knew who would be the focus of all the mudslinging.

Duy's voice rose. "Our country faces Cambodia. In the North, too, we face invaders, and who is it we face there?"

He paused for effect. Nobody answered, though I could see Hung eagerly mouthing the word *China*.

"I'll tell you who it is we face," exclaimed the Youth Leaguer. "China armed the Cambodians. China attacked Lang Son. It's China, always China."

Hung and his friends again turned around and peered at me. I returned their looks as steadily as I could. At the end of the talk, Hung and the other two boys followed Duong and me out of the room.

"Did you learn anything in there, Tra?" sneered Hung.

Duong stopped to face Hung but I kept walking. As he caught up with me, Duong hissed, "What's wrong with you. Why don't you stand up to them?"

"Have you noticed how they always walk with their heads bowed, these people?" called Hung. "My father says they were like that in the American war, always slinking around, up to no good."

Duong turned and retorted, "And what did your father do in the American war?"

Hung's eyes narrowed. "What's that? What did you say?"

I gripped Duong's arm. He was on dangerous ground.

"Go on," said Hung. "Say what you mean. Has our Chinese brother here been spreading lies? You've been listening to Tra too much. I'm sure my father would like to hear what you've got to say."

"Forget it," I whispered. "You'll get both our fathers into trouble."

Duong stared at me, then at Hung, then pushed past our tormentors.

Hung shouted, "What's wrong? Not feeling so brave now?"

I was seething. Duong was angry, too, but fortunately, Hung and his friends had had their fun and were walking away. I turned to Duong. "What did you mean about Thuan?"

"Don't you know? Thuan worked for both

sides in the war. My father told me. I bet he got paid by both sides too."

I stared at Duong, unable to believe what I had just heard. The most powerful man in the village was a crook and a traitor!

"You may be right," I said cautiously. "But don't lose your temper. That's just what Hung wants."

Duong nodded. "I'd better go home now," he said.

"I'll see you later," I called after him.

As I crossed the road, I saw Oanh trying to turn a buffalo to the left. She grinned at me and said, "Hello, Tra. They should put a reverse gear on these vehicles, shouldn't they?"

Oanh was in our class and she'd been at the talk. It seemed that Hung and Duy weren't doing that well in poisoning minds against me. I helped turn the buffalo in the direction he was supposed to go.

Oanh smiled. "I won't have to do this much longer," she said.

I gave her a questioning look. Laughing gaily, she made a waving motion with her hands, then trotted after the buffalo. I remembered what Duong had said: "They're all leaving."

Grandmother was serving the evening meal to Mai on the veranda. As usual it was rice with nuoc mam, a spicy fish sauce. I glanced into the house and asked, "Why are we eating here, Grandmother?"

Grandmother looked up and replied, "Bao's here. He wants to talk to your mother."

Bao, my mother's elder brother, and Mother were the only children of my grandmother to survive the war. Two other sons had been shot by the Americans. Her eldest daughter was buried beside my grandfather in the rice fields. They had been on their way to the market one day when a mine blew up beneath them.

I was curious about Bao's visit. He worked for the district administration, the new government. His job had something to do with the fishing fleet down the coast. I had already guessed that this wasn't a social call.

I strained to hear what Bao had to say to my mother, but Mai kept pestering me to make shadow creatures with my hands. I could only catch snatches of conversation.

"It's getting bad at work," said Bao. "They're always talking about my Chinese brother-in-law. There are two younger men who want my job. They're very ambitious, and they know that they can undermine my position by mentioning Loc. I'm sick of it all."

I heard my mother's voice, very low and anxious, but I couldn't hear what she said.

Mai began tugging at my sleeve. "Do a chicken. Go on, do a chicken for me."

Then I heard Bao again. "They've sent these two Northerners to take charge. They're not happy with the way we've been doing things, and it's got even worse since they arrived."

"What are you supposed to be doing wrong?" Mother asked.

"We're not getting enough gold from the boat people. That's right—we can let them go, as long as they hand over their gold. We just close our eyes to it. Did you know a couple of top Party members have left as well? It must be bad if they're clearing out."

I heard my mother say, "What can Loc do? They just won't leave him alone."

Bao replied, "Tell him to keep his head down. There's talk of suspicious activities. It's nonsense, of course, but when you hear them talking about suspicious activities, it means arrests."

I must have been listening a little too keenly. Grandmother tapped me on the shoulder and said, "I know what you're up to. Pay attention to your meal and leave the adults to their business. Children today! When I was a girl I wouldn't have dared to be so impudent!"

I couldn't imagine Grandmother being a good, submissive little girl, but I kept my thoughts to myself. I resigned myself to eating and entertaining Mai. There was nothing else to learn from the conversation inside the house. Grandmother saw to that.

Bao and Mother came out onto the veranda. Bao said, "So you're back, Tra. How have you been spending your afternoon?"

I grimaced. "A boy from the Youth League gave us a lesson," I said. "It was about China."

"It would be," said Bao, scowling. "Still, we shouldn't have to put up with that much longer."

With that, he climbed onto his little motorcycle and kick-started it. As he rode off in a cloud of dust, I wondered what his last remark had meant.

Underground

▼

"You row," said Duong.

I guided the sampan toward the forest. Duong never wanted to row anymore. He just talked and talked about Hung, and getting even. I let him talk. His words became part of the afternoon's music, along with the lapping of the water, the scraping of the insects, and the call of an Indian cuckoo—"Ko-el, ko-el."

"How did you get away from Lanh?" I asked.

"I didn't have to," said Duong. "She's having a dress made."

We climbed to the tree line where the rusting tank stood as a landmark. At our approach, dozens of swifts took to the air in a storm of tiny beating wings. I watched them wheeling about us for a moment, then I turned to Duong.

"Are you sure about this?" I asked.

"You sound just like my sister," he said, raising his eyebrows.

I stared at the forest with its many shades of green—from almost black to blazing emerald. What had life been like for the men who had fought here year after year? But Duong wasn't interested in dwelling on such things; he just wanted to explore those mysterious tunnels.

"I came prepared this time," he exclaimed as we traced our path past the strip of defoliated land that cut across the forest. He unwrapped a rolled cloth he had been hugging all along the way. It contained an oil lamp. "This should light our way."

I followed him to the spot where he had uncovered the tunnel door. Duong knew exactly where it was. Brushing aside the dust and rotting leaves from the wooden hatch, he slipped his fingers into a ring and pulled it up.

He lit the lamp, then crouched by the dark hole. "Here," he said. "Pass it down to me when I call."

He swung for a moment, grinning, then he dropped into the tunnel below.

I handed the lamp down. A moment later Duong shouted, "Well, what are you waiting for?"

I breathed deeply, then lowered myself into the tunnel after him.

"Which way shall we go?" Duong asked excitedly.

I looked at the yellowish glow stretching along the dirt walls of the tunnel. Overhead, I could make out logs set into the roof to reinforce it. "I don't know," I replied, doing little to hide my doubts about this adventure.

Duong smirked and led the way. I had to crouch slightly beneath the curved roof. The fighters who used this network of tunnels must have spent days on end without straightening their backs. There was little to see other than long stretches of tunnels cut into the reddish earth.

Suddenly Duong stopped dead.

"What is it?" I asked.

"A snake. Look, there it is."

"Shall we go back?" I asked hopefully. "It could be poisonous." It didn't look poisonous, however. It was small, yellowish, and dozing, but I hoped it would be enough to put Duong off. It didn't.

"Let's try along here," he said, illuminating another branch of the tunnel. "If there's nothing down here, we'll go back."

I was relieved by his reply. My feeling of unease had been growing with every step I took.

"Hey! Look at this!" gasped Duong, as he peered around a bend in the tunnel. It revealed a large, open space. The roof was supported here and there by wooden props. There was evidence of the tunnel's occupants strewn about on the floor: a shattered crate, a fragment of a map, a tin can, a lamp lying on its side.

"I bet they planned battles here," exclaimed Duong, moving forward into the chamber. "Come on," he urged. He wanted a witness to his discovery. "I'm sure there's more. Yes, look...."

Suddenly he shrank back, brushing against me.

"What is it?" I asked.

There, in the light of the oil lamp, I caught sight of a bundle of old rags.

"Can't you see it?" he cried.

I took the lamp from Duong and leaned forward. The bundle of rags covered the remains of a human body. I could make out the bones of a hand. I dropped the lamp, plunging us into darkness.

"Get it! Get it!" cried Duong.

I scrambled on the floor, terrified of what I might touch as I groped for the lamp and relit it.

"What do you think it is?" asked Duong.

"I don't know—a soldier maybe," I suggested. I held the lamp out in front of me.

"Don't go any closer," whispered Duong.

I took no notice. I had glimpsed something beside the body and my curiosity was stronger than my fear. I edged forward, trying not to look at the body. Duong gripped the sleeve of my shirt. I pushed him away and reached down. My fingers touched a package.

"Let's get out of here," pleaded Duong. The discovery of the body had knocked all the boldness out of him, and our roles were suddenly reversed. I stepped away from the body and held the package up to the light.

"Come on," groaned Duong. "Bring that with you if you want, but let's get out of here. Now!"

He snatched the lamp from my hands and led the way, almost at a run. I could see him shaking as he hauled himself out of the trapdoor.

"I can't believe what you did back there," he said.

I watched Duong clawing at the hatch. I searched inside myself. Why wasn't I that scared? Back on the surface, I examined the package. It was a sheaf of papers, sealed in a polyethylene bag.

"How can you?" asked Duong. He was staring at me if I were less than human.

"You won't catch anything from it, you know," I said. "There's nothing to be afraid of."

The moment I said the word "afraid," Duong changed his tune. He became self-conscious, and fear loosened its grip.

"Okay, what's in it?" he asked.

I tugged at the wrapper. There was a photograph of a young man and woman and a three-page letter, which had an address somewhere in the North.

Inside the letter was a scrap of paper which read: "The Americans are overhead again tonight. I can feel the earth shake as they walk above me. They know I'm here. I don't expect to survive. If I'm dead when you find me, please send this letter to my mother."

Water must have got into the wrapper, because parts of the letter had been reduced to a blue stain. I was only able to make out fragments.

"Read it out loud," urged Duong.

I began to read:

> The jungle has become my home. I carry all that I have on my back. It will be three years soon. It is hard to live so long away from you all. I did not dream that it would be like this when I came south to fight for the fatherland. Now, I dream of home, of you and Binh.

"It's a soldier down there," said Duong.

I ran my finger down the page until I came to another passage I was able to decipher.

> I thought I could put up with anything—the jungle, the leeches, days with little or no food, even the fighting, but it's the bombers I'm afraid of. I'd never imagined the terror I felt during a B-52 raid last night. The jungle was on fire.

Shrapnel mowed it down. All of us are terrified. There is nothing we can do but endure.

I broke off. "I wonder how anyone could live through that," I said.

Duong ignored me and snapped, "What else does it say? What else?"

I continued:

I have made a good friend and comrade. He's from Saigon. We talk at night of our dreams. He wants to be a doctor. We share everything. I am lucky to find such a friend in the middle of war.

I could read little in the rest of the letter. It ended: "Hold my darling Binh for me."

"What are you going to do with it?" asked Duong.

"Keep it."

"Why?"

I shrugged my shoulders. I folded the letter and resealed the wrapper. I simply said, "Let's go home."

As we walked back toward the sampan, dusk was falling, and the night herons were beginning to stir from their colonies in the trees. Duong allowed me my silence.

Hero

———————

"Where did you find this? Where?"
My father's voice wrenched me from
my sleep. I rubbed my eyes. It was early, just after dawn. The sun was still low in the sky, its
first rays barely clearing the gloom inside the
house. A gecko scuttled across the floor at
Father's approach.

I looked up at him. I was confused, hardly
awake. He looked agitated, in a way I had never
seen before. Whatever was in his heart remained
there, hidden from the eyes of others.

"Wake up, Tra. I must know. Where did you
find this package?"

Father's voice softened as he saw the fear in

my eyes. His voice was urgent, insistent, but coaxing rather than harsh. "Did someone give this to you? Who was it? I must know. Come on, Tra. Wake up. This is important."

"In the tunnel. I found it in the tunnel, by the body."

"Body!" exclaimed my father. "You found a body?"

"Yes," I said shakily as I sat up. "Duong and I found a tunnel in the forest. You know, where the NLF fighters hid during the war. We didn't mean any harm. We were just exploring when we found the body. The letter and the photograph were next to it, so I picked them up and brought them home. I didn't think I was doing anything wrong."

Father's eyes were hard. "You must show me this tunnel, Tra. We'll go today."

"We'll need a boat," I said. "It's across the waterways."

"I'll get you a boat," said Father. "Are you sure you'll find it again?"

"I think so," I said. I got dressed as quickly as I could.

Father began shoving things into his canvas bag. He said something to my mother as he got ready, then tapped me on the shoulder.

"It's time to go. I will see Hoan about the boat."

I rowed the sampan out toward that now

familiar tree line. As I moored it, I glanced at Father's tense face. He was impatient to find the tunnel entrance. I couldn't remember him being in such a hurry before. From time to time as we climbed toward the forest, he asked, "Are you sure this is the way?" or "Are we nearly there?"

Finally we reached the spot. I brushed away the earth with my hands and uncovered the hatch. "This is the way in," I said.

"Show me the body. I've brought a light."

Father was excited and angry. I'm sure he wasn't angry with me, but I was nervous. He seemed coiled, as if ready to strike, and it didn't matter what at. He pulled up the hatch and flashed the light inside.

"Now, show me," he ordered.

As I led him along the tunnel, he was at my shoulder, urging me forward. He didn't once look at the walls or the ceiling of the underground pathway. He treated it like a walk through the village.

"There's a bend just ahead," I said. "The chamber is beyond it." Father looked first at me, then ahead into the darkness.

"You go first," I said.

Father looked at me again. For the first time that day, he gave me a smile—as if he had just remembered how young I was and how frightened I must be. As we emerged into the chamber, I pointed. "It's over there."

Father took a few steps forward while I hung back. He knelt down by the body. His face was masked by the shadows, but I could see that he was deeply troubled. Suddenly, I heard him say one word—a man's name—"Nam."

Father produced a cloth from his bag. He unfolded it and began to wrap the body in it. I couldn't look while he gathered up the remains and bound the body in the sheet. Then he said, "Tra, take my bag and the light. Lead us back to the surface."

I did as I was told. I was glad to be in the open air again. All I wanted to do now was go home, but I was to be disappointed. Father began digging a hole in the forest floor. I stared as he worked. He was digging a grave.

When it was finally ready, Father slowly lowered the body into it and hauled himself out. He stood for a moment, gazing down at the improvised burial shroud, then he began to shovel earth over the body. I listened to the thump of the earth, wondering why this body was so important to my father. Had he known the man he was now burying?

When the earth had been replaced, Father pulled a piece of wood from his bag. It had been part of a crate. He sat down and began to carve into its surface. Then he hammered the makeshift headstone into the ground by the grave.

I read the inscription. "Liet Si"—hero. My

father stood by the graveside for a long time, staring at the shabby plot of earth in silent respect. I looked from his thin, tired face to the inscription—hero. Though he was silent and wrapped in his own thoughts, I had never felt closer to him.

After a long time, Father ran a hand over his face, as if surfacing from his own inner world.

"Tra," he said, "I have to return to the tunnel. Will you be all right here?"

"Of course I will," I answered.

"You must wait right here. Don't wander off."

Father disappeared into the tunnel. I sat by the hatch and looked around me at the rich green ocean of the forest. I listened to the scraping of the insects. I thought of the letter we had found in the tunnel and tried to imagine the B-52s overhead, the whistle of the bombs, the shrapnel destroying the forest. The ghosts of war still haunted this place.

I paced the ground, impatient for my father's return, and read over and over again the simple inscription on the headstone—hero. What if I had been Nam's age during the war? Would I have fought? No matter what was happening now, I still loved my country. Yes, I surely would have fought. I could now be lying out in a jungle grave, far from my family. I shuddered.

As the afternoon wore on, I hovered uneasily around the tunnel entrance. I was becoming anxious. Where was Father? What if he was lost? What if those earthen walls were to collapse, trapping him in their terrible darkness? I even considered feeling my way along the tunnel. I pictured myself groping through the cloaking darkness and found myself saying again and again under my breath, "Where is he? Where is he?"

Finally, as all sorts of terrors crowded my mind, Father reappeared. First he thrust his canvas bag out of the hatch. Then, a moment later, he hauled himself out by those strong, wiry arms of his. I looked curiously at the bag. Had he found something in the tunnel? What did he have in the bag?

"It's time to go," he said, in a way that told me I mustn't ask what he had seen in the maze of tunnels.

We walked back to the boat. As I drew the oars up ready to push off, I plucked up the courage to ask, "Did you know him, the dead man?"

"Yes," answered Father, "I knew him. I recognized him the moment I discovered the photograph by your mattress."

"Was he a friend?"

"Yes. He was the greatest friend I ever had in my whole life."

"Was he a good man?" I asked.

"Yes," replied Father in a dull, tired voice. "He was good, and he was brave. He should never have died alone down there."

I rowed steadily toward the village, as Father looked out across the paddies. "How do you know that he died alone?"

"I just know," came the murmured reply.

"Were you a soldier too?" I asked.

Father didn't answer this time. He had spotted Hoan waiting on the bank and waved to him. I had the feeling he was glad of the interruption. As I followed him out of the boat and onto the dusty path toward the village, Hoan's conversation broke the spell of the afternoon. He was talking to Father about the latest villagers to leave Vietnam. I recognized their name. It was Oanh's family.

Hung

"Grandmother," I asked, "you supported the NLF in the war, didn't you?"

Grandmother was inspecting the few poor vegetables she had carried home in her basket.

"Yes, I supported them," she replied. She shook her head at the vegetables and added, "For all the good it has done."

"What do you mean?" I asked.

"Thirty years of war," said Grandmother. "Thirty years, and what have we got to show for it? A lot of bodies in the ground, good men and women who died for their country."

"Aren't you proud of them?" I asked.

"Proud? Of course I'm proud. My own husband and three of my children died in that war. I'm proud, but I'm also angry. What did they die for? This country is dirt poor. Everywhere people are leaving. I never dreamed it would end like this."

"The Youth League says the Americans won't let us recover from the war. We can't get aid."

"Maybe that's right, but something is very wrong here and it can't just be the Americans taking their revenge. Officials are making money while others go hungry. They all want their palms crossed with gold. There's corruption everywhere. Have you heard about the power lines?"

I shook my head.

"It's a terrible scandal," Grandmother explained. "People have been tapping the state power lines for cooking. Somebody on the village committee has been taking bribes to close his eyes to it. Men from the government have come to investigate."

I looked into Grandmother's face. She saw that I was waiting for her to say more.

"Questions!" she exclaimed. "With you it's always questions. When I was your age, I would never have been allowed to ask such questions."

"Maybe you should have," I replied.

"You're certainly your father's son," sighed Grandmother.

Before I could ask what she meant, she continued, "Our family didn't support the resistance because we were told to. We listened to what the NLF had to say and it made sense. They said the puppet government of the Americans was giving all the land to the landlords. They said the NLF would give us democracy, land to the tillers, improved living conditions for the people. Where are their promises now?"

I interrupted her. "What did you mean—I'm my father's son?"

Grandmother smiled. "You never miss anything, do you? You're a thinker, young Tra, and a dreamer, just like Loc. I can see you in 10 or 15 years' time—you'll be just like him. I just hope you don't suffer for it as he has."

"I think Tra should go and play with his friends," called Mother. She didn't like the turn my conversation with Grandmother was taking.

Grandmother gave her a sidelong glance, then rubbed her palms on her cotton trousers. "Meals don't make themselves, Tra," she said. "Find somebody younger to talk to. Look to the future, not the past."

I was furious with Mother. Why did she have to turn up just when I was learning something new? I stomped away toward Lanh and Duong's house.

As I reached their veranda, a familiar old army truck rumbled noisily into view. Sitting next to the driver was Thuan, and next to him Hung. I glared at them as they passed. The truck came to a halt by a broken-down bamboo fence, and Thuan and Hung jumped down. While Thuan marched into a house, Hung loitered outside, returning my gaze with obvious hostility.

"Where's your father today, Tra? At the fishing village again?" he called.

I wondered where his questions were leading. "Yes, he's working on an engine," I replied.

"Working? Is that what you call it? Since when do you Chinese work? I thought you were all spies and fifth columnists."

I tried to ignore him.

Hung called out again, "It's funny that your father is always repairing fishing boats lately. Are you thinking of going somewhere?"

I turned and walked over to Hung. "What do you mean?" I demanded. I felt hot and agitated.

"You know."

"What do you mean?" I repeated, gripping Hung's shirt.

"Think about it," said Hung. "Why would he always be working on a fishing boat? All you Chinese are doing it—abandoning Vietnam."

"You don't know what you're talking about," I shouted.

"Don't I? My father says Loc is being watched. The village committee knows what he's up to. They've got him marked down for suspicious activities."

Suspicious activities! I'd heard that before,

from Uncle Bao.

"That shut you up, didn't it, Chinese brother?" sneered Hung.

I didn't even try to reply this time. I clenched my right fist and struck him hard on the lip. He looked shocked, but he recovered quickly from the blow and hit me on the temple. I felt a dull pain and was dizzy for a second. Hung grabbed at my shirt and hit me again, in the chest. I held on to him, then managed to kick him just above the knee.

I'll never know who would have won the fight. I felt strong hands grip my shoulders from behind, then I heard Hoan saying, "Stop it. Stop it this minute, you two."

Duong and Lanh were watching. I wondered how much they had seen and felt slightly ashamed of myself. Mother always said that anger made you look foolish. I would have looked even more foolish if I had taken a beating for my fit of temper.

Hung sneered at me again and walked over to his father, who had come hurrying out of old Mr. Hao's place.

"What's the meaning of this?" squealed Thuan in that high-pitched voice of his. He looked at me and his eyes narrowed.

"You," he said. "You're Loc's son. So it's come to this, has it? He's gone so far as to poison children against authority. It will do him no good, you know. I won't be put off. I'll watch your father until he slips up. Then I shall have him. You see if I don't."

With that, Thuan climbed into the truck, and Hung followed, grinning broadly in triumph.

"What was that all about?" Hoan asked as the truck pulled away.

"Hung was insulting my father. He says we're going to run away, but we're not. We're not!"

Hoan looked troubled. He stared at me for a moment, then he called to Mr. Hao, an old man with sunken cheeks and clear, sad eyes, "What did Thuan want?"

"My land," said the old man simply.

"Your land?" Hoan repeated. "What do you mean?"

"He wants me to grow fruit. I told him it isn't suitable, but he says I have to. Orders."

Hoan was angry. "That's crazy," he snapped. "We know what to grow and what not to grow. What does Thuan know about farming? Orders! All we hear these days is 'orders.'"

While Hoan grumbled, Lanh and Duong came over to me.

"Are you all right?" asked Lanh.

"Yes, I'm fine," I murmured.

"To think that you're the one who told *me* not to lose my temper!" said Duong.

"Hung said we were going to run away," I explained. "We wouldn't run away. We just wouldn't."

"There's nothing wrong with leaving," said Hoan, joining us. "If there's a better life elsewhere, why not go?"

"But it's our country," I cried. "People have died for it."

Hoan lowered his voice and said, "Yes, and they gave their lives for nothing."

I stared at Hoan. "You can't mean that."

"Why not?" asked Hoan. "You don't even remember the war. Why does it matter to you so much?"

I wanted to tell him about the body in the tunnel, about Father planting a headstone reading "hero" on the soldier's grave, but I knew I couldn't. I just said, "They can't have died for nothing. They just can't."

Hoan's eyes were sad, and he made no attempt to convince me. He rested his hands on Lanh and Duong's shoulders and said, "I believed in taking sides once, a long time ago, but I've seen where it leads. All I want to do now is to bring up my family the best way I can. I'm just not sure I can do that here any more."

The Veteran

————

I watched Grandmother placing fruit and sweets on the little wooden altar in front of our house. She was explaining to Mai that the food was for the spirits of our ancestors. Incense perfumed the air as Grandmother knelt by the altar.

At the sound of footsteps, I looked up through the smoke of the incense. There, in front of me, was Duc. I knew him at a glance. He was a short, stocky man with silvery hair and metal-rimmed glasses that made him look like a doctor or a teacher. I was to learn that, in a way, he was both.

"Can it be? Yes, it must be! It's Mai and Tra, isn't it? Have you grown so much in less than a year?"

Mai looked bewildered. She barely remembered Duc's last visit during the Tet holiday. I remembered, though. I remembered the mischievous way he smiled.

"Where's your father, Tra?" he asked, peering into the house.

"He's working on the boat," I answered.

"That's good, that's good," observed Duc.

I examined his face closely. He seemed to know about Father working on the fishing boats, but how did he know? And why did he seem so relieved to hear about it?

"Will he be long?" asked Duc, looking around.

"No, not long," said Grandmother.

"So you can spare fruit for your ancestor, Sang. You could make a fortune on the black market in the city, you know."

I almost burst out laughing. I rarely heard anyone speak to Grandmother like that, using her personal name.

"The black market is for scoundrels," muttered Grandmother.

"Yes, and for people who can't get things any other way," said Duc with a sly grin. He coughed a little and then said, "Tra, where is your mother?"

"Gone to see Uncle Bao, I think," I answered.

This information also seemed to please Duc. "I'll take a rest now," he said. "Will you call me when Loc returns, Tra?"

I nodded. Grandmother watched Duc disappear into the house. She smiled. "Rest!" she said. "Only a city dweller could talk about resting." But she said it in a way that betrayed her fondness for Duc. He was as different from Grandmother as you can imagine, but I knew they liked and respected each other.

When Mother and Father arrived home half an hour later, I ran to meet them with the news of Duc's visit. Even before I opened my mouth, Duc was on the veranda, calling, "There you are. We must talk."

I joined them on the veranda, and, to my surprise, I wasn't told to leave. Ignoring my presence, Duc and Father quickly began to talk.

"They took me in for questioning, Loc," said Duc.

"When did they come? How long did they hold you?" demanded Father.

"It was last week," said Duc. "They released me after two days, but it shook me, Loc. It really shook me."

"What did they ask you?"

"What do you expect? Was I spying for China? Who else was involved?" Duc was talking rapidly, passionately. "I thought I could put up with anything—all the rumors, the insinuations, even the arrests. But to call us criminals—we who fought for the fatherland!"

Father noticed me for the first time. He said,

"Is this what you wanted to hear so much? They're treating us like the enemy. Look at this man. Your uncle fought the Americans, and the French before them."

"I knew it!" I exclaimed. "I knew it wasn't true what Thuan and Hung have been saying. I knew you weren't a traitor."

Father ran his fingers compulsively over the table. He seemed to find something funny in what I had said. "Do you see, Duc? It's here, too. They try to make a scapegoat of us. They even try to set our children against us."

Duc leaned forward. "What did we fight for, Loc? What?"

"Lower your voices, you two," said Mother, suddenly rising from her place in the corner. She pointed at me, then said to Father, "Think of your children. What if somebody hears you, somebody who can't be trusted?"

Father placed his hand on Duc's shoulder as he rose. "She's right, of course. We can't afford this reckless anger. We must be careful."

Duc gripped Father's wrist, and replied in a hard, cold voice, "The time for being careful is past. You must know that. They're watching all of us. They have loaded all the country's problems on our shoulders. It has to be now. If we delay, we both face arrest."

My blood froze in my veins. "What does he mean? Delay what?"

"Haven't you guessed, Tra?" said Father. "We're going to leave."

"Loc!" cried Mother. "You said we wouldn't tell the children until it was time."

"It's like Duc says," Father replied wearily. "The time for being careful is past. We must not delay."

I stared at him. Hung was right. We were running away. Hung and Thuan had won.

In a corner of the house, I sat on the floor with my back against the wall. I felt confused. Why did we have to flee and leave Vietnam to the likes of Thuan?

All around me, preparations had begun for a hurried departure. Duc's arrival and the threat of arrest hanging over my father had hastened the family's secret plans. Grandmother uncovered hidden stocks of rice. Mother bundled up our modest possessions. Father gathered his books and his tools. And all the time, Mai stared at the urgent rummaging with her dark, wide eyes.

From time to time, Father peered out into the dusk. At last, as the darkness gathered around the house, he said, "There are arrangements to be made. I won't be long."

I sat for a long time with my arms resting on my knees and my face buried in my folded arms. I felt a hand on my neck and looked up.

Duc smiled and asked, "What's wrong, Tra?"

"I don't understand it," I said. "Why are we running away? Is it because of Father?"

Duc looked puzzled. "Because of Loc? What do you mean?"

"Nobody will ever talk about Father's past," I replied. "What has he got to hide?"

Duc sat beside me. "Such wild thoughts in the mind of one so young! Loc has nothing at all to hide."

"So why must we leave?" I cried. "A boy at school said we were leaving. I told him he was a liar."

Duc shook his head. "It's not easy for us to leave, Tra. Your family suffered terribly in the struggle to free Vietnam, but we were willing to make sacrifices for freedom. This isn't the Vietnam we fought for though. We didn't struggle all those years for a country strangled by poverty and corruption. We've merely exchanged one tyranny for another."

"But there must be another way. You're just giving up!"

Duc looked into my eyes. There was a hint of anger in his. "You must never say that, Tra. Let me try to explain. I joined the resistance to the French when I was a young man. In 1954 I thought our dreams were fulfilled when we defeated the French at the battle of Dien Bien Phu."

"Everybody knows that," I said.

Duc ignored my interruption and continued.

"I settled in the North. They were in urgent need of doctors, so I resumed the career I had given up to fight for my country. I thought I could live in peace in a free land, but it wasn't to be. The Americans took over from the French, and South Vietnam and North Vietnam were plunged into yet another war. I thought it was time for younger men to shoulder the burden of freeing their country, so I decided not to volunteer to fight. Then one day...."

Duc's voice trailed off, but after a moment he went on. "One day in 1967, I was returning home to my wife and son. The loudspeakers announced an American bombing raid. I hurried toward my house. I had to make sure that my family was safe in the air-raid shelter. As I ran down the street, I heard the PA system announcing the approach of the bombers. 'Now the planes are 60 miles from us. Now they are 30 miles from us.' They dropped napalm. By the time I reached the front of my home, it was on fire, a direct hit. My wife lay dead on the steps. I tried to reach my son in the burning house that had been flooded by liquid fire. I saw something like a blackened doll....It was my son."

I glimpsed the pain in the teary eyes of the former soldier, and I began to understand why there had never been much talk of the war in our home.

Duc continued, "In the town, they erected a

stone of hate—a statue to protest the bombing. There was no shortage of volunteers to trek south through the Truong Son Mountains to fight the Americans. I joined the young men as they made their way down the Ho Chi Minh Trail. They needed people like me to go to South Vietnam to work for liberation. I began by visiting my brother, Loc's father, in Cholon. I began to win recruits for the struggle against the Americans. One of them was your father, Tra."

"But how can you leave after all that?" I protested.

"You must understand," explained Duc. "I've given 30 years of my life to a cause. I believed that if we drove out the foreign powers, Vietnam would be free, but now...." Duc stared at the ceiling.

"I was ready to suffer at the hands of the enemy," he continued. "But to suffer persecution at the hands of our own countrymen, that's betrayal."

Our conversation was interrupted by the sound of footsteps on the veranda. He pressed a finger to his lips. "Can it be Loc?" he whispered to my mother.

"He can't be back this soon," she replied.

"Then who?" said Duc, clearly anxious. Nobody answered him. Everyone's eyes turned toward the door.

There was a light tapping on the bamboo door,

then a pause, then the tapping was repeated—louder and more insistently.

Grandmother said, "I shall have to answer it, for good or ill."

She opened the door slowly. In the darkness I could make out the shadowy figure of a man. Grandmother stepped outside to talk to the night visitor. I heard her whispering. A moment later came the man's muffled reply.

There was a catch in Grandmother's voice as she suddenly exclaimed, "The escape! But how did you hear about that?"

The Boat

Grandmother ushered the man in from the darkness. It was Hoan.

He looked around the room, his eyes falling on Uncle Duc for a moment. Then he said, "It was a guess really. I was sure Loc was up to something. Well, will you take us with you?"

"Who is this man?" asked Duc sharply.

"Hoan," replied Grandmother. "A neighbor."

"Can he be trusted?" asked Duc, as if Hoan wasn't in the room.

"I've kept your secret thus far," interrupted Hoan.

"He can be trusted," replied Grandmother. "And he has a sampan. It would be safer to reach the fishing village by the waterways, rather than on foot. Couldn't we find room for him?"

Duc acknowledged Hoan for the first time and asked, "How many in your family?"

"My wife and two children, Duong and Lanh," replied Hoan.

"Loc has planned our provisions carefully," said Duc doubtfully.

Hoan was almost pleading. "I have some rice and vegetables, a little fresh fruit and some water bottles. I too have been planning, you see, ever since I realized what Loc had in mind."

"You haven't told anyone else?" asked Duc.

"No," replied Hoan. "But if I could guess what was happening, there might be others."

Duc frowned and said, "I will talk to Loc when he returns."

It was an hour before Father arrived home. The sight of Hoan sitting in the corner of the room didn't seem to surprise him, but he looked troubled. He didn't even try to keep secret from Hoan where he had been. There were evidently bigger problems than discovery by Hoan.

"What's wrong?" asked Mother.

"The official that Bao has been dealing with— he's swindled us," replied Father.

"How?" asked Duc.

"We paid him everything we had. Four taels of gold for each person, that's what he said. For that he would arrange that the security police turned a blind eye. Tonight I discovered he has accepted payment from other families. He's told anyone who asked him about escaping that we would take them. We always knew we had to keep the numbers down to ensure our safety. Now we have to pack 40 people into one boat. It's madness."

"Forty-four," said Duc.

Father glanced at Hoan. "I knew that was why you were here. Well, why not?" he said despairingly. "Four more, what does it matter? I've already told Thang and his family that they could come."

"When do we leave?" asked Mother.

"Tomorrow night," Father answered. "Bao is arranging everything. He has to pay one of the fishermen for an auxiliary engine."

"Who are these other people who are coming with us?" asked Duc.

"I don't know," Father replied. "At least one family is from Ho Chi Minh City. That's all I know."

"Let's hope they can keep their mouths shut," said Duc. "The authorities will move against us for certain if they know we're leaving. And you?" he barked, turning to Hoan. "Can you keep your mouth shut? Can your family?"

"You can trust me," said Hoan. "My family's safety is at stake."

Duc looked Hoan steadily in the eyes. There

was a cold resolve about my uncle. His wry humor had evaporated with the events of the night. Everything had been stripped away, leaving a man determined to survive at any cost.

He rested a hand on my father's shoulder and said, "It appears that we have no choice. We leave tomorrow."

The next day was strange. It was a day of waiting and tension, knowing we were leaving, but not being able to tell anyone. Father and Duc left early for the fishing village to ensure that nothing went wrong at the last moment. They were suspicious of the fisherman who had sold them the boat and of the official they had bribed to let us go. Mother and Grandmother were anxious too, mainly because so many of us now had to keep the secret of our departure. They had planned all along to keep it from us until the very last moment. Now they had to wait and hope. Grandmother didn't leave Mai's side all day. She couldn't trust my sister not to let something slip.

As for me, I hung around with Duong and Lanh. We found it difficult to talk to each other. All we could think of was the journey ahead and what the future held for us out there in a strange world across the sea. Most of the time we just sat in silence or walked the dusty paths of the village.

We were crossing the rickety bamboo bridge

that led to the village at the south end when we met an unwelcome sight. Waiting for us on the other side were Hung and three of his friends. I winced at the thought of more taunts from them.

"Is your father at the fishing village again, Tra? There must be a lot of work to do down there." Hung spoke with his usual sneer.

Duong spat back, "At least Tra's father works. What does yours do? He takes what others have sweated to drag from the soil, that's what."

I heard Hoan's words on the lips of his son. Duong was angry. Lanh and I knew that he might say anything if Hung got under his skin.

"Why do you never speak up for yourself, Tra?" called Hung. "Like father, like son, eh? Get some idiot to do your fighting for you. With Loc, it's that blockhead Hoan. With you, it's his brainless son."

Duong was beside himself. He stepped off the bridge and faced up to Hung. "Shut your mouth, Hung. Shut your mouth right now."

Hung laughed and said, "I don't keep quiet about the truth. Remember, Duong, you're Vietnamese. Why are you hanging around with this Chinese spy?"

Duong yelled, "Don't call him that. You know nothing. I'll be glad when I don't have to see your ugly face again...."

Duong realized he had said too much and fell silent.

Hung peered into his face and said, "And when do you think that will be, Duong?"

Duong tried to brush past but Hung blocked the way. "You're not thinking of going on a voyage, are you?"

My throat tightened. He knew!

"You are! You think you're getting out, don't you?"

"You don't know what you're talking about," snapped Lanh, tugging at her brother's arm. I followed her as she dragged Duong down the path. Hung stretched out his foot, sending me sprawling in the dust. I stood up quickly and turned to face Hung. Fortunately, I felt Lanh's hand restraining me gently.

I turned reluctantly, burning with shame and indignation at having to walk away. As I caught up with Duong, I could hear Hung shouting, "Did you learn your lesson last time, Tra? Look at him—he's shaking in his boots."

Hung's cronies were laughing. I scowled and walked on. Lanh said, "You did the best thing, Tra. It would be bad for us all if you lost your temper and gave us away."

"I know," I said, "but I just want to show him! It hurts to have to put up with his insults."

"It would be worse to see your father in jail," retorted Lanh.

Duong kicked at a stone and said glumly, "I wish it was time for us to leave. I can't think of anything else."

I turned my eyes to the patchwork quilt of rice fields. I would soon be leaving this landscape forever. "What do you think Hong Kong will be like?" I asked.

"Free," answered Lanh.

"And rich," said Duong. "Everybody lives in big houses with electricity and running water. They drive around in cars too. I can't wait."

When we finally made our way back to the hamlet, I saw Grandmother letting Phao out of the corral. As I reached her side, she said softly, "That will be the last time I let him out to roam."

"Are you sad to say good-bye?" I asked.

Grandmother checked that there were no unwelcome listeners. Then she said, "Sad? Yes, a little, but Phao's only a buffalo. It's your grandfather I remember. I can see him now with the little calf. It doesn't seem that many years ago. Why, it feels like only yesterday."

Grandmother watched Phao plodding away, twitching his tail at the flies. Then she wiped her hands on her cotton trousers and walked into the house.

I reached my mother's side. Mai was drooped next to her in the hammock on the veranda.

"Is Grandmother very sad?" I whispered.

"Yes," said Mother. "It's important for her to be close to her ancestors. At first she refused to come, but in the end she couldn't bear to be parted from us. We're all she has left. I'm worried about her, though. She knows nothing apart from life in the village."

As we waited for Duc and Father to return, we ate a little rice and vegetables, gathered up a few possessions, and put them in bags, which we hid. Nobody bothered to light the oil lamp as it got dark. We just sat silently in the blackness.

At last the moon emerged from behind a cloud and flooded the trees with its pale light. And there, etched against the moonlight, were Father and Duc.

"All ready?" whispered Father.

No one replied to his question. He didn't expect anyone to. It was more of an instruction. We followed Duc toward the waterway that ran alongside the paddies. Father went to fetch Hoan and his family.

Once everyone was installed in the sampan, Hoan began to row. Trembling leaves hung over the water and brushed my cheeks as we slipped through the darkness. A bat flitted overhead.

I looked back just once, but the hamlet was already out of sight beyond a curve in the waterway. Mai began to cry softly, but as Grandmother comforted her, she nodded off to sleep.

Mother was crouching over Mai to put a blanket over her shoulders, when a bright, cruel light burst through the palm fronds.

I winced as I heard Thuan's high-pitched voice.

"The boy definitely said they were leaving, you say?"

"Yes, Father. I heard him."

Hung! He had passed on Duong's careless talk.

Hoan waved for us to lie flat. He bent low himself, pulling us to the bank by an overhanging branch. The beam of light raked the forest and illuminated the trees, beneath which we were hiding. I glanced at Duong. He looked scared out of his wits.

"Can you see anything?" shouted Thuan.

The voices of two, maybe three men replied, "Nothing."

"Let's try their house, then. You'd better be right about this, Hung."

As the voices faded into the night, Hoan pushed off. Nobody spoke much after that. We sat peering anxiously about us. The forest had become something to be feared.

At last we reached the fishing village where we would board the boat. Duong asked his father, "Do you think we'll ever come back?"

Hoan was at a loss for words. It was Grandmother who replied, "There's an old saying: The leaves always fall back to the roots of the tree. No matter where he goes, a Vietnamese must always return home."

Mother and Father exchanged glances. I could tell by their eyes that they didn't believe we would ever return.

Leaving

It was midnight by the time the last of the passengers, a plump little man from Ho Chi Minh City, came on board. From time to time he would beam and put on a show of gaiety that hardly suited the occasion. I still remember his first words. As Hoan helped him on board he gave a false smile and said, "So here we are on the boat to freedom. America, Ford motorcars, Pepsi-Cola!"

Hoan scratched his head, and Duc smiled as he watched the man stagger past the people huddled on the deck of the boat.

The new arrival sat next to me and looked around. "Is this first class?" he joked. "First class to freedom, right?"

I looked at Mother, then back at the new arrival. Most of the people on board were quiet and apprehensive. The newcomer's voice carried the length of the boat.

Father emerged from the enginehouse and he too stared at my neighbor.

"Mr. Manh," said the little man, standing up to introduce himself.

With a cloth, Father was rubbing oil from his hands.

"I have...had a shop just off Tu Do Street. The very best merchandise, of course. I take it you are the captain of this vessel."

Father stared blankly at Mr. Manh, then said, "Captain? I think you have the wrong idea about this journey. I can patch up an engine but that's about it. If we're lucky I can hold this wreck together as far as Hong Kong. There...." Father pointed to a thin, ailing man standing in front of the enginehouse. "That's the nearest you'll get to a captain. Quan there is a fisherman, but he's never been more than a few miles out to sea, much less all the way to Hong Kong."

Mr. Manh mopped his forehead with a delicate handkerchief. Then he beamed his wide smile and said, "Of course, how silly of me. This is a great and arduous journey indeed, but when did freedom come easily?"

Father returned to the enginehouse, and Mr. Manh again sat down next to me and said, "He seems a very able man. Yes, very able indeed."

"He's my father," I said.

"Ah, your father," said Mr. Manh, weighing the importance of this piece of information.

"Who's that?" said Mai as she woke with a start.

"Just another passenger," said Mother, stroking Mai's hair.

A moment later, Mai was asleep again, settling against Mother and rocking slightly with the motion of the boat.

"My sister," I said.

"Your sister," repeated Mr. Manh, with the same show of deep interest.

The throbbing of the engine grew louder. Father appeared again and murmured, "We're leaving."

People instinctively looked back at the fishing village and the distant, dark lines of the hills.

Hoan called to me, "So it's begun, boat boy. It's begun."

I rested my head against my knees.

Boat boy! I'd been so proud of the nickname. Now it gnawed away inside me like a sickness. We were leaving the only home I'd ever known. Vietnam wasn't just earth and trees and people to me. It was the way I felt and thought. It was all of me. How could I leave it?

As I fell asleep, I could hear Mr. Manh chuckling. "Boat boy. That's what I call a good omen. Yes, that's very good indeed."

It must have been shortly after dawn when I woke up the next morning. Most of the people were still doing their best to sleep. Some were sprawled full-length on the deck, while others were curled up against the enginehouse or the guardrail of the boat. A few seabirds circled above in the hope of finding a few scraps. Somewhere behind me a baby was crying, and its mother was trying to comfort it.

In the light of day, I realized just how shabby and fragile our little vessel was. Paint was peeling everywhere, and some of the wooden planks were rotting. I glanced at Mr. Manh. His head was thrown back, and he was snoring at the back of his throat.

"A city dweller," observed Grandmother.

"I didn't know you were awake," I said.

"I didn't sleep much," she replied. "I've been listening to him half the night. He talks in his sleep, you know."

"What did he say?" I whispered, hoping Grandmother would follow my example.

She didn't. She simply said, "All I could hear was America, America, America. He says Pepsi a lot, too."

Grandmother moved closer and lowered her voice. "Be careful what you say, Tra. We're among strangers here."

I felt like protesting that it was Grandmother who had been talking loudly.

"There are two families from Ho Chi Minh City. I heard them cursing the Communists," said Grandmother. I stood up, and almost fell back down again.

Grandmother smiled and said, "It's the way you were sleeping. You must have been lying on your leg."

I felt foolish, but didn't really mind. "Do you know where Father is?" I asked.

"Yes, there's a meeting going on to organize life on the boat. Can you see?" Grandmother pointed round the side of the enginehouse. I walked over to the group of men gathered there— Father, Hoan, Duc, Bao, the fisherman Quan, and another man I didn't know. I listened as they talked about keeping watch, water rations, washing and toilet arrangements, medicines, and what to do if there was illness.

Eventually, the meeting broke up.

"Tra," said Father, "can't you sleep?"

"It's light. I wanted to look around."

"That's easily done," said Father, indicating the cramped conditions. "Come with me."

He led me into the enginehouse. I expected a conducted tour of the boat's engine. Instead, Father whispered, "Duc told you we were NLF?"

"Yes."

"Never mention it. There may be passengers who fought on the American side. They would blame us for their plight if they knew."

I nodded. Father smiled, then said, "Off you go now."

When I made my way back to the family, Mai was jumping up and down over Mother's legs. The game kept her happy for a while, then she sat sulkily between Mother and Grandmother.

"Did you come far to join the boat?" asked a voice.

It was Mr. Manh. His face looked creased and puffy with sleep.

Mother said, "No, not far."

"I came from Saigon," said Mr. Manh. "I mean Ho Chi Minh City. I keep forgetting that they renamed it after the war."

"You were right the first time," interrupted a voice. It was one of the men Grandmother had pointed out. "We can say it now—Saigon."

I felt uncomfortable. I exchanged glances with Thang, who had just joined us. He smiled and glanced at the speaker.

"They could force us to live their way, but in here...." The man tapped his temple. "Yes, here I remembered Saigon as it was, before the Communists wrecked everything."

Thang frowned. He didn't care for such talk.

I stared at the water. It was like being taunted by Hung all over again, hearing things you disliked but having to hold your tongue. Was there nowhere my family could feel at home?

Mr. Manh leaned forward and said, "But now

we're on our way to freedom. I want to go to any freedom country, but best of all America. Yes, America. I remember the GIs with their Pepsi and American cigarettes."

I half expected Grandmother to say something about their guns and their bombs, but she didn't. She just gazed impassively across the sea.

Thang eyed Mr. Manh and sneered, "Pepsi! Is that all you can talk about? We ought to call you Pepsi."

"Pepsi," said Mr. Manh delightedly. "Yes, from now on you must call me Pepsi."

As I listened to the drumming of the engine through the planks of the deck, and to Pepsi's excited voice, I wondered where freedom for us would be. I stared at the waves. The voices of the people on the boat faded, and I felt as if I were drifting away from them.

I looked up and saw a pelican, brilliantly white against the cloudless, azure sky. It hung on the currents of air and swung out over the gleaming sea. This is your element, white bird, I thought, not mine. Boat boy? No, I'm not at home here, cast onto a lonely sea.

"It's a pelican, isn't it?"

It was Father. "Yes," I said. "It's beautiful."

"You'd like to be like him, wouldn't you, Tra? I always felt like that when I was a boy. Parents clip your wings. You don't just look like them. You also inherit their struggles and their enemies."

I looked at Father. He seemed to be saying that he was sorry for something. I turned my gaze on the crowded deck behind us. Father smiled, glad to see that I was too cautious to ask him to say more.

We watched in silence as the pelican wheeled before beating its wings briskly and sweeping away into the distance.

People were beginning to busy themselves, washing clothes or preparing a little fish and rice. The dull routine of the journey had begun: washing, slopping out, distributing skimpy rations of fresh water, eating, and most of all, simply watching.

An Encounter

◆

"I want a shop, a little shop," said Pepsi. "Oh, and a car to see America—the Grand Canyon, the Statue of Liberty...."

"Shut the fool up, somebody. Shut him up, for God's sake!"

Pepsi looked hurt by the former official from Saigon, a man called Vu.

"Sit down," said Vu's wife. "You're making a fool of yourself." Vu scowled and resumed his place.

With the passing days, people had become irritable. Many lay in a listless stupor, some half-dead with seasickness brought on by hour after hour of buffeting from the high waves. Wrapped in spray-drenched blankets on the open deck, we had got used to our fitful, exhausted sleep. We never felt clean or refreshed but just dozed, too weary to sit up and talk, too cramped and uncomfortable to sleep properly. Quarrels broke out with increasing regularity. It seemed as if there were always children whimpering. The salt irritated our skin, and babies cried helplessly.

I overheard another conversation. It was hard not to, since we were packed together like sardines. I was never able to get used to the fact that we were in the middle of a vast, unchanging expanse of sea, yet we felt hemmed in. It was crazy. Everywhere we looked there was open space, yet we couldn't walk, or exercise—we couldn't even stretch our arms.

"We sold everything, even our gold wedding rings, to escape. I would have given anything to get out. Look at me, just look at me. I fought to save my country from the Communists, and now...."

I looked at the speaker. He was as thin as a toothpick.

"Four years I was in the camps. I came back to find my family on the streets, my children living on salt and pepper. And for what? All I did was to fight for my country."

"I'll tell you why you got locked up," shouted Vu. "You didn't kill enough Viet Cong, that's why."

I winced as I remembered that old Ro had told me Viet Cong was what the Americans called the NLF. I searched in the faces of Duc and Father for some sign, some reaction to this exchange, but they remained expressionless.

It was the same every day—the stories, the complaints, the hopes, and the dreams. There were those who had served in the military or the government of the defeated South. There were the Chinese. There were the peasant farmers with their desperate yearning for a better life with food in their bellies, clothes on their backs, and a decent home.

I turned back toward the sea. On the horizon I glimpsed something.

"Look out there," I called. "Look, there."

Duc walked over and followed the direction of my pointing finger. "Where? I can't see anything."

"There!" I cried. "Oh, look! You must see it! It's another boat!"

"He's right," said a woman. "There is another boat."

Duc hurried forward to the bow. Turning round he called, "Bring her over. There *is* a boat."

As we approached, we could see that it was another fishing vessel, barely half the size of ours. Everyone had been complaining that we had to put up with such a fragile vessel, but that tiny boat was something else again. It really was madness to try to cross the sea in such a raft.

"What do you think happened to it?" I asked. "It's empty."

"I don't know," answered Duc. "Heavy seas, a typhoon maybe. Let's take a look."

Duc and Bao began to lash the small boat to ours, and Bao clambered aboard it. There wasn't a soul to be seen. It was completely deserted.

Everyone on our boat pressed against the guardrail.

"Where are all the people?" asked Lanh.

Bao turned to face us and shrugged. "Who knows?"

As the words left his lips, we heard a muffled sound that seemed to come from under a tarpaulin. Bao tossed back the cover. He stared for a moment, then reached under it and drew out a little girl about Mai's age. She struggled fiercely in Bao's arms, then stared at him with eyes that didn't seem to understand what was happening. I'd never seen such a look on anyone's face.

Mother reached out and took the girl from Bao. She stroked her hair to calm her. The girl drew back, staring with the same uncomprehending look in her eyes.

"Where are your parents?" asked Grandmother.

The child stared up at her but didn't say a word.

"She'll speak in her own good time," said Mother.

As Bao continued to inspect the boat, something about his face made me uneasy. I couldn't have been alone, because Vu called, "What's wrong? You've found something, haven't you? Tell us what's wrong."

Bao glared at Vu and retorted, "There's nothing."

"I don't believe you," said Vu. "I'm coming to see for myself."

Bao's expression changed from anxiety to alarm. Before Vu could climb over the guardrail, Father gripped his arm and said, "He told you there was nothing."

"Let him go," said another of the Saigonese. "What are you hiding?"

Others raised their voices in support of Vu. Bao ran his hand over his face and said, "So you want to know, do you? You really want to know? Well, there's a woman lying under this tarpaulin. Her throat's been cut. There's another body hanging from a rope over the side. Now are you satisfied?"

A stupefied silence fell over the crowded deck.

"But who would do such a thing?" cried Mother, looking down at the child in her arms.

Mother's question went unanswered. Duc helped Bao wrap one body in the tarpaulin and threw it into the waves, then cut down the other body.

We all watched silently, but before any of us

could discuss the meaning of this grim discovery, we heard Quan cry out, "Look! There's a junk! They're coming back!"

"They?" asked Pepsi. "Who are they?"

"Haven't you guessed?" said Quan. "The people on this boat were murdered by pirates." The fear in Quan's voice was unmistakable. He looked at the junk's sail with wide, staring eyes.

Somebody began to cry. Children sensed their parents' anxiety and began to whimper.

"Get down!" whispered Father. "Everybody get down. They might just think we're the boat they've already raided."

Bao and Duc scrambled back aboard our boat and joined Father in helping some of the bewildered passengers back to their places. We flung ourselves to the deck, mothers and fathers desperately covering their children.

"It's no use," said Quan grimly from his hiding place behind the enginehouse. "They're coming closer."

I squinted against the sea spray. Quan was right, the junk was approaching. I could just see the crew. They were looking for signs of life.

The junk closed in steadily. I could hear the pirates' voices and the sound of weapons being made ready. They were going to board us. I felt a ball of fear choking my throat.

Suddenly there were footsteps behind me. I looked up to see Father brandishing a rifle and shouting in the direction of the junk.

"Where did he get a rifle?" murmured Duong, his voice betraying a mixture of surprise and admiration.

"Who knows?" said Thang from his place behind us. "Just be thankful he has one."

I listened as my father and the pirates shouted angrily at each other.

"Let us board," said a voice.

"Take one step aboard this boat and I fire," yelled Father.

I heard the pirates arguing among themselves. "Crazy man," they were saying.

"What's happening?" whispered Pepsi's thin, soft voice. "Won't somebody tell us what's...."

The hostile eyes of the people on either side of him cut him short.

"Let us board, or we'll sink you," the leader of the pirates threatened.

"Try and I'll kill you," cried Father.

At last I heard Quan sigh with relief. "They're giving up," he said. "They're after easier prey."

People began to emerge from their hiding places to watch the junk sail away.

Hoan stared with amazement at the rifle. "You've got a gun!"

Father weighed it in his hands and said proudly, "Not just any old gun. This is the Kalashnikov AK-47 assault rifle."

He spoke of it almost like a friend. He returned the astonished looks of the people on deck and added, "There are just a couple of problems. It isn't loaded, and it doesn't work anyway. The firing mechanism is completely corroded."

Some people laughed—either at the absurdity of facing the pirates with a useless rifle or with sheer relief. Vu wasn't laughing, however. Instead, he was staring at the rifle in Father's hands.

His voice interrupted the relieved laughter. "What are you doing with a Viet Cong weapon?"

Father turned. He looked shaken.

"You were one of them, weren't you?" Vu continued. "You were VC."

Duc gave a nervous laugh and said, "Don't be a fool. What would he be doing here?"

But Vu wasn't to be diverted. "What's wrong? Wasn't Communism good enough for you? That's right. You got a nasty shock when you won, didn't you? Your new world's turned into a nightmare."

Pepsi tried to intervene. "This can't be right. Surely a Communist wouldn't leave?"

"Where have you been?" said another Saigonese. "They're all leaving. They've been falling out among themselves. One of their leaders fled to China just before we left."

I stared at Father. Why didn't he say something? Surely he could have come up with an explanation. I was angry with him. It was as if he wanted to be found out. I needed him to speak out, to stand up for himself the way he had to Thuan.

Father turned away, but Vu blocked his path. "You and your kind murdered my son. He was shot by the VC, and do you know why? He translated for the Americans. He wasn't even in the army—he was just a teacher. They shot him simply because he worked for the Americans for a few hours a week."

Father's eyes didn't meet Vu's bitter, accusing stare. A moment before, Father had been a hero. Now at least half our companions were watching him in stony silence.

Hoan's voice broke the silence. "What's wrong with you all? Loc saved your lives, didn't he? Can't we forget the past?"

"He's right," said Quan. "If we start squabbling, none of us will survive. I don't give a damn for your politics—I left all that behind in Vietnam. I just want a decent job and a quiet life. I don't take this boat any farther until you all get back to your places."

People slowly sat down. Only Vu remained standing. His wife was trying to coax him back to his place, but he just stood and stared at Father. The look in his eyes chilled me to the core.

The Storm

That night the weather broke. Wrapped in blankets that were soon wet through from the steady rain, we spent a sleepless night. Everybody seemed to have the same thought—"What if the pirates return?" But my mind was filled with a different nightmare. Each time I searched among the other passengers for Vu, he was staring fixedly at Father.

The sea was swelling. Quan grimaced and said, "If the pirates have any sense they'll be long gone. We're on the edge of a storm."

"Will it be long before it hits us?" asked Father.

Quan scanned the darkness and said, "We may avoid the worst, I don't know. All we can do is hope."

Rain swept across the sea all the next day and the waves got bigger. People could barely eat or drink. The salt water had ruined most of our food, but occasionally we would gulp down a few drops of fresh water. While most of us lay wretchedly in our wet blankets and listened to the drumming of the rain, Quan and Father took turns steering the boat. I saw them swallowing instant coffee powder to keep awake. They never took their eyes off the mounting waves—and Vu never took his eyes off Father.

As darkness fell for the second time since we had encountered the pirates, Quan bellowed against the strengthening wind. "If you value your safety, find something to hold on to. Better still, tie yourself down to something."

Even as he spoke, the wind was driving the rain across the boat in heavy sheets. I glimpsed the blank, unchanging face of the girl we had found. She barely blinked as the rain ran over her eyes.

I wondered what those eyes had seen, but my thoughts were shattered by a wave that rose in an instant and almost lifted the bow into the air. I looped a rope over the guardrail and hung on. I could see a woman desperately trying to shelter a young baby. Then a sharp cry made me turn.

"Mai!" yelled Mother.

I caught sight of my sister being swept over the side by a great wave that broke upon the deck in a vast explosion of spray. I wrenched myself loose from my rope and staggered toward her. To my relief, she had managed to cling to the guardrail. As I reached out to her, I felt a thump in my ribs. Grandmother, too, was struggling to Mai's side and had been thrown against me.

"Hold on there, Tra. I'll need somebody to take her from me."

It was an order, and I obeyed. I watched as Grandmother clambered over the side. I held on to her as she slid her arm around Mai's waist.

"Let go!" she cried suddenly. "I can't get her if you keep hold of me like that."

I relaxed my grip on the old woman's sleeve. Grandmother edged lower, clinging to one of the rubber tires that had been tethered along the side of the boat. With a huge effort she bundled Mai back over the side. I reached forward and hauled Mai, coughing and gasping, to safety. As I turned to reach out to Grandmother, I heard a loud, grinding noise. The other boat was being thrown against ours by the waves. I saw its bow rising sharply out of the water.

"Grandmother!" I screamed.

She raised her face to see the bow come crashing down upon her. Mai screamed. I opened my mouth, but I couldn't even make a sound. For a second I saw Grandmother's black cotton shirt among the white-flecked waves. Then she was gone.

Mother reached my side and stared into the sea.

"I couldn't help her," I cried. "I'm sorry, I'm sorry."

Mother couldn't force out her words. She just hugged Mai and me, and wept.

Father joined us. He glanced at the little orphan girl, now sitting alone where Mother had left her, then at us and said, "What are you doing? Don't you know it's dangerous? Get back to your places."

"It's Grandmother," wailed Mai. "She's gone."

Father frowned. He didn't understand.

"A wave swept Mai overboard," I explained, tears running down my face. "Grandmother pulled Mai back, but the other boat crushed her."

Another wave crashed onto the deck and sent all of us sliding against the enginehouse. Father grabbed a loose rope and lashed it to the guardrail. "Hold on to this," he said and pulled himself into the enginehouse.

Quan was shouting something, but I couldn't make it out. Seconds later he was beside us yelling, "The bilge pumps aren't clearing the water. Start bailing."

People began bailing with anything they could lay their hands on.

A crash of splintering timber sent Quan racing back into the enginehouse. He reappeared, staring wildly. He shouted above the roaring wind, "Where's Bao?"

Bao stumbled toward him.

"We're breaking up. Can you take a line over and help people onto the other boat? I don't think this old hulk will survive the storm."

Bao did as he was told and tied a thick rope to the other vessel's mast. Crossing would be hazardous. With each swell of the waves the two boats pulled apart, then closed again, the two hulls grinding deafeningly against one another. Duc and Hoan braced themselves against the guardrail and began to pass the children over to Bao.

Bao called, "I need someone else to help me."

One of the peasant farmers sprang across the gap between the two boats. He was a man of about 60, and his agility didn't match his courage. He lost his footing and slipped between the hulls as they closed again. He was pulled clear just before the boats crashed together.

Reemerging from the enginehouse, Father stepped forward and held back the peasant. He shouted, "Let me try," then waited until the two boats closed again and stepped across to stand beside Bao. I saw the pain on his face as he put all his weight on his bad leg.

The passengers formed a line and readied

themselves to step over the gap between the boats as it narrowed. Each time Duc and Hoan shouted, "Now!" someone else would make their way over. I followed Lanh and watched her jump across the gap into Father's arms.

"Get ready, Tra," called Bao. I stared as the distance between the boats closed. They looked like the jaws of a dragon, a dragon that had devoured my grandmother. I could be its next prey. Even in the cold, drenching rain I felt hot—as if I had a fever. I was overcome with fear of the dragon. Bao reached out but I drew back. The jaws separated, and I stared into the dark waves.

"What's wrong?" yelled Bao. "Why didn't you jump?"

I was too afraid to speak and tried to move back down the line of people waiting to go. As I turned, I saw the faces of the other passengers. Their eyes were what I noticed. No matter how old they were or how seasick they had been, they were desperate to save themselves—to get off the capsizing vessel. They all wanted to live.

"Are you all right, Tra?" cried Father. "Do you want me to come and get you?"

I blinked the rain out of my eyes and looked at him, waiting to catch me. I could see the unmistakable signs of pain in his face. He must have gone through agony jumping between the boats with his crippled leg. It was in him, too, this unfailing thirst for life. I couldn't let him down, I couldn't let myself down.

"Now!" cried Father. "You've got to jump now!"

The dragon's jaws were closing, but I'd lost my fear. I hurled myself forward and fell into Father's arms.

"Don't blame yourself for Grandmother," he said. "The two of you saved Mai. That's what Grandmother wanted."

No sooner were the words out of his mouth than there was a second huge crash. The two boats lurched, hurling people across the decks. A wave burst over the boat, tossing the orphan girl like a doll and sweeping her along the flooded planks.

In a second Pepsi was scrambling on his hands and knees like a child playing dog. He seized the girl and crawled to safety.

"I don't think she has suffered any harm, Madam," said Pepsi in that strange, affected manner of his, as he returned the child to Mother.

Suddenly the boats lurched again. Pepsi lost his balance and fell into the sea. Quan leaned out from the other boat and dragged the little man to safety. I heard Quan say, "Heroes shouldn't die that easily."

Once more the boats tipped and lurched. Bao called over to the handful of people left on our old boat, "Come on! You've got to get off now."

But the boats were lurching so much that no one dared move.

As his boat's bow rose above the waves and swung viciously toward us, Quan bellowed, "It's too late. We're cutting loose. If we don't, we'll both go down."

With that, the fisherman swung a machete and hacked through the ropes binding the two vessels. Once the boats were cut loose, they drew away from each other. I tried to look through the clouds of rain, to see the people who remained on our old boat. Pepsi knelt exhausted on the deck. Quan was plunging back into the enginehouse to see if he could hold the boat together. In the lashing rain I could make out a dozen or so other shadowy figures, but I only recognized one of them. Vu was leaning forward against the guardrail, staring at my father. I shall never forget his eyes, burning with hatred through the storm.

"Will they survive?" asked Lanh.

"That's for the sea to answer," replied Hoan. "I just hope they stand a better chance with fewer people on board."

I looked around me at the wretched figures huddling together. Bloodshot eyes stared helplessly into the storm. Though I hated myself for it, I was grateful that I could no longer see Vu's among them.

Freedom

The storm seemed to rage for days, but it was late the next afternoon when the high winds finally began to ease and dozens of fish arched over the waves like sweeping birds. It was as if they were emerging to announce that life could resume after the terror of the storm. I heard something thump against the hull and looked down to see several fish with round heads and black, shiny skins.

"Pigfish," said Father with a grin. He, too, was enjoying the improving conditions. "They're as stupid as people who cross the South China Sea in a fishing boat."

I found it hard to return his smile. I was thinking of Grandmother out there beneath the waves.

"That girl we found, she spoke earlier," said Father.

"What did she say?"

"Not much. She cried mostly. She still can't believe what she saw. She told your mother that the pirates killed everybody. The child's mother hid her under the tarpaulin, otherwise she'd be dead too. Her name's Phuong."

"What will happen to her?" I asked.

"I don't know. Your mother thinks we should say she's part of our family. Life might be bleak for a little orphan girl in a foreign land."

I grimaced. I wondered if life would be much better for any of us. Somehow, I wasn't sure if I believed in Pepsi's idea of freedom.

"Do you want to take the steering pole for a while?" asked Father.

I took it without a word.

"Are you thinking of Grandmother?"

"Yes."

Father left me to my thoughts and sat next to me with his chin resting on his chest. Not a soul stirred or spoke. I reached down and touched Father's shoulder.

"Are you awake?" I asked quietly.

"Yes. What is it, Tra?"

"Tell me...about your war."

Father shook his head slowly, then rose and drew close to me. He looked at our sleeping companions, then began to speak in a low voice. "I suppose it is time I told you. It all began when I was a medical student. The students were getting caught up in protests against the government. They believed that the president was only able to stay in power with American backing. The people didn't want him in office. Friends of mine, especially the Buddhists, would say, 'Come with us. Don't you love your country? Don't you want to get rid of the Americans?' I tried to keep out of it. My father hated politics, and so I did as he asked and kept clear of the protests."

"What changed?" I asked. "Something must have changed. You did get involved, didn't you?"

"Yes," said Father. "I got involved. One day Duc arrived. I admired him. He'd fought the French, and now he'd returned to Saigon to organize matters among the Chinese community in Cholon. He had bitter quarrels with my father. I always sympathized with Duc. Even Duc's arrival wasn't enough to get me involved, though."

"What did?"

"The protests became more bitter. One day a student friend of mine came running up to me in the street. 'Have you heard?' he cried. 'A monk has burnt himself alive to protest American involvement in Vietnam. How much longer can you stand aside?'

"That was the last straw. I joined Duc handing out leaflets and recruiting people to the liberation struggle. I joined the National Liberation Front—" continued Father, "what the government called the Viet Cong. I read pamphlets that proclaimed that 'nothing is more precious than independence and liberty.' Such ideas fired my imagination. Soon, I was arrested by the authorities. I'd been reckless. I had more courage than common sense then. I was beaten and questioned. After my release, Saigon was too dangerous a place for me to stay, so the NLF sent me to the jungle. They decided I would make a good commander. I was young and ready to make any sacrifice they asked of me, but it was a hard life. We were poorly armed at the time, and sometimes I felt like a hunted animal. We relied on the good will of the villagers for food and shelter. A young boy joined our unit one day, a Northerner by the name of Nam."

"Nam!" I exclaimed. "You said it in the tunnel."

"That body was my friend Nam. When he came south down the Ho Chi Minh Trail, he was fresh out of school—just a kid. We became friends from the very beginning. We shared everything, even food and water. Nothing was more important than your comrades. We stayed up all night talking, exchanging photographs of our sweethearts, dreaming of our future. One day Vietnam would be reunited as one country. It would be independent and free and not dominated by foreign powers—a true democracy. We would live happy, prosperous lives and visit each other's families during the Tet holiday."

I listened to Father describing his dream of a free and independent Vietnam, then glanced at the wretched huddle of refugees. How had it come to this? I kept my thoughts to myself and asked, "What happened to Nam? How did he end up in that tunnel?"

"I don't know exactly, but I can guess. Nam and I became veterans of that struggle. It was hard—you can barely imagine just how hard. The Americans and the South Vietnamese army launched search-and-destroy missions. We suffered terrible losses. The enemy had aircraft, helicopters, limitless supplies of weapons. It seemed that everyone in our unit was wiped out every few months, only to be replaced by new recruits. Only Nam and I survived. The other men said we were invincible."

Invincible! The image of the body in the tunnel filled my mind. It was hard to believe that it had once been a strong young man.

"You said you could guess what happened to him?" I said.

"Nam? Yes, I can guess. He and I commanded our unit. During the Tet holiday in 1968, the order that we had been waiting for came: *dong khoi*—the general uprising. The NLF and the North Vietnamese army launched an offensive against towns and cities all over South Vietnam. We believed that the people would rise up alongside us and drive out the Americans and their puppet government. Nam and I led our men against an American base. They were thrown off guard at first, then they counterattacked. We lost most of our unit in the battle. They say now that Tet was the beginning of the end for the Americans. Yes, that's probably true, but for me it was a tragedy. All my friends died during the Tet offensive."

"But Nam didn't die there, did he, in the battle?"

"No. At last they forced us to retreat into the jungle. We got away. Helicopter gunships saturated the area with gunfire. Then the bombers came in, lighting up the sky with flares. The earth shook from the bombs. It felt as if your heart would burst. Well, we survived. We found a sampan and drifted downriver. One night, we left the sampan and began to make our way across land. As the moon came up from behind the trees, I saw figures in the forest. I flung myself to the ground as the shooting began, but I felt something hit my leg. A moment later I heard Nam firing his AK-47. He yelled to me to run. I couldn't, but I managed to half-hop, half-limp with my wounded leg. Nam covered me until I reached the edge of a rice paddy. I tore my shirt off and used it to stop the bleeding. I must have passed out."

A baby began to cry and her mother rocked her gently. Father paused before continuing, "The next morning when I woke, I looked up into the face of a woman. It was your grandmother, Tra. She took care of me, and I owe her my life. While I was recovering, she smuggled food to me. Some days it was Sang, some days it was your mother. They smuggled rice to me in the bamboo handles of tools. Sometimes suspicious American officials stopped them, but they couldn't pin anything on them....In time I recovered and took up the struggle again."

"You went back!"

"Yes, the struggle was everything to me— everything."

I couldn't imagine believing that strongly in anything. What good had it done him?

"I was in the jungle, fighting, but I married your mother secretly. Every few months I would return in the night to see her, to see my new son."

"But you don't believe in the revolution anymore?" I asked.

"I believe it has been betrayed, but that doesn't mean it was wrong to fight for what I believed in."

Father indicated some of the sleeping passengers. "They were betrayed too. Some of them supported the revolution. Look what it has done for them."

"When did it all start to go wrong?"

"I don't know. It took time. I became aware of a whispering campaign against the Chinese, even while the war was going on. I couldn't understand it. Hadn't we given our lives? Then...."

He paused for a moment, then continued, "One day I was given an order to kill an NLF member who had been giving information to the Americans. My heart was in my mouth as I approached her home. I'd done terrible things before, but I'd always told myself it was for a greater good. I just didn't believe that anymore. My victim sat up in bed as I entered her house. I saw immediately that she was pregnant, and I couldn't do it. I ask you, how could I kill a pregnant woman? I just walked away from the war that night and returned to your mother. I tried to retreat into my own family, to get on with my own life. I had given enough.

"But to this day it haunts me. I want to leave it behind—it was all such a long time ago—but I dread it catching up with me. Did my failure to obey orders make me a deserter, a traitor to be shot like a dog? That day when I stood up to Thuan, I kept thinking, what if he finds out?"

"And Nam?"

"I never saw him again after that night. He was reported missing in action. I hoped he'd survived, but I didn't really believe it. They must have trapped him in that tunnel. When I saw his body there, it confirmed what I already knew in my heart. My dreams were finally dead. It was time to get out."

Father paused, then said, "Nam saved our lives, you know. It was his gun I pointed at the pirates. He would have liked that. He would have appreciated the joke."

I smiled. "I know where you got the gun. I knew you'd found something in the tunnel."

It was Father's turn to smile. He patted my shoulder, then said, "Get some sleep. I'll take over now."

I asked a last question, "Did we really have to leave?"

"Yes, we had to. For Duc and I, staying would have meant being arrested. Many Chinese have been caught in the purges. For the rest of the family it would have meant poverty. I had dreamed of prosperity and freedom, but we weren't going to have either. I couldn't condemn you to a future like that."

"But now Thuan and Hung have won."

"Won?" said Father. "What have they won? A country half-strangled to death by poverty? They've won nothing!"

For a whole day after my long talk with Father, I felt as if a new chapter had begun in my life. The lack of sleep, the seasickness, the constant bickering didn't seem to matter. But another day dawned, then another, and my optimism drained away. The miserable routine of the voyage began to choke me. What was worse, we had begun to run out of drinking water. Were we going to die after all? Had we been spared by the storm only to die of thirst? Those were my thoughts as I slipped into another restless doze.

"A ship! A ship!" Duong's voice shattered my sleep.

He was right. There, between the crests of the waves, I could see it, a grey container ship.

Father was struggling with the steering pole and trying to guide us toward the ship's path. He began yelling at people to sit down, but they were too excited. They were jumping up and down frantically waving their arms. To judge by the position of the sun, it must have been late afternoon. I couldn't believe I had slept that long.

Father almost shouted himself hoarse, trying to get everyone to sit down. "Keep still," he pleaded. "You're making it impossible to steer."

Bao and Duc stumbled along the deck, trying to control the shouting, waving people, but it was no use. They were close to hysteria.

"Don't go," pleaded Lanh as the ship grew more distant. "Please don't leave us." She sank to her knees. Watching her, I realized how wretched we had become.

Some, disbelieving, continued to call after the ship. Most, like me, slumped back in their places.

Since the storm had faded, a terrible stillness reigned. A vast, orange-red sun wreathed by ribbons of grey cloud was sinking below the horizon. Soon the sun was gone, leaving behind an eerie afterglow on the waves. A pale moon rose, illuminating tiny fish that looked silvery in its light as they leapt out of the water.

In a little while, I felt someone pressing against me. It was Father. He had finally surrendered to the exhaustion of long hours of steering the boat. I eased his hand off the pole, then lowered him into my place. It seemed as if he were now the child and I the man. I stood upright and held the steering pole straight. I looked ahead into the night.

At first I couldn't believe my eyes. Ahead of me, laid out like an enormous jeweled carpet, were hills and islands dotted with the flickering lights of villages, and beyond—a great city. Skyscrapers climbed darkened hillsides. Neon lights flashed and pulsed. It must have been there all this time, like a mischievous spirit, waiting for us to notice.

"Hong Kong," I murmured.

Duong was the first to stir. "What did you say?"

"Hong Kong," I said. "It's Hong Kong."

A second later we were screaming like a couple of madmen, "Hong Kong! Hong Kong!"

Mai took up the chorus, "Hong Kong!"

Soon everybody joined in, shouting or whispering it excitedly. I could see people's faces gleaming with joy in the moonlight.

Hoan said one word, "Freedom."

Father's eyes met mine.

"Is it?" I whispered.

"I hope so," he said, "I do hope so."

A quarter of an hour later we were blinking against the glare of a searchlight. It played across the sea and blinded us. Voices were shouting harshly in English and Chinese, voices that belonged to strange, dark figures whose faces we couldn't see. Could they really be helping us, I wondered? It was as if we had reached not just another country but another world. I read the lettering on the launch that met us—Royal Hong Kong Police.

As we were hauled on board, the despondent silence of the previous days gave way to excited chatter. Was I the only one to be worried by our welcome? Hoan was the last to climb aboard. He looked like a little boy, hugging his wife and Lanh and Duong in turn.

"Freedom," he said again.

One of the policemen was drinking a can of cola. Hoan reached for it and said, "We lost a friend by the name of Pepsi. You'll let me toast him, won't you?"

Whether the policeman understood Hoan or not, he reacted harshly, pushing Hoan's hand away and half-drawing his billy club. Hoan's face registered shock and fear as he fell heavily on the deck. The other refugees stared in disbelief. For the first time, I was able to distinguish the features of the policemen. Most of them were Chinese, and their eyes were cold—even hostile. There was also a European who seemed to be in charge. He was barking orders and pushing aside the bewildered passengers who approached him to ask for food and water. Arguments were breaking out between refugees and policemen.

Ignoring Uncle Duc's repeated questions about milk for the babies, the European said to his second-in-command, "More mouths to feed. Why can't they just go back home?"

Vu

▼

Phuong and Mai met me with broad smiles when I returned to my bunk area.

"What's up with you two?" I asked. "Your birthday was last week, Mai. It can't be that."

Mai laughed out loud. "Birthday! No, we're not celebrating my birthday."

I frowned. She was eight now but she still acted so young sometimes. It horrified me to think about our time in the refugee camp. Like so many other Vietnamese, we had crossed the South China Sea in search of a new life, only to end up in barbed-wire cages bulging at the seams with desperate people. How could we have lived for the last two years under such conditions?

144

My bunk was on the third tier of the steel platforms that ran the length of an old warehouse. Below me were Mai's bunk and Phuong's, and below
theirs were Mother's and Father's. A makeshift
partition of blankets separated us from Bao's
family just a couple of yards away. Duc and some
other single men lived on the other side of us.

Lines of washing hung the length of the steel
platforms, and the smell of cooking filled the
airless building.

"What is it, then?" I asked. "You're grinning
like a couple of idiots."

I didn't like surprises, and the arrival of the
last batch of refugees a fortnight ago had brought
one. It had brought Vu.

"Guess," teased Phuong.

I lay down on the mattress and snapped, "I
give up."

"Father's done it!" cried Mai. "We're leaving!"

I sat bolt upright. "You don't mean it."

"It's true," said Phuong. "We're going to
Canada."

I could scarcely believe my ears. This was the
news we'd all been longing for. "You're quite
sure, quite sure?" I asked.

"Yes," chorused the pair.

"I wonder what he told them," I said.

"Does it matter?" laughed Phoung. "I don't
care what he told them. We're going to get out
of this place."

I scrambled down. "I'm going to tell Duong and Lanh."

"They know already," squealed Mai with delight. "They're getting out too. You're the last to find out."

I was grinning myself by now, but my pleasure didn't last long. Out of the corner of my eye, I saw him, the way I'd seen him so many times in the last two weeks. Vu was in the doorway, just standing and staring, watching me.

"What is it?" asked Mai, noticing the change in my expression.

"It's him again," I whispered.

"Ignore him," said Phuong. "He's a bitter old man who's still living in the past. What can he do to us?"

I left Mai and Phuong and walked down to the beach. Vu followed me a few yards behind. He worried me. Why, of all those we had lost in the storm, was he the only one to succeed at the second attempt to escape Vietnam? Where were Quan and Pepsi? The last Vu had seen of them was when they were blown back to the coast of Vietnam and arrested by the security police.

I turned away from Vu and crossed the sand. The beach was the only place in the entire camp where I felt free. Though I could still see the steel fences and the rolls of barbed wire, here at the water's edge I had friends—the row of boats. The beached boats reminded us all of the journey we had made to get here. Some of them were "holed." Their occupants had smashed through the hulls so that the police couldn't tow them back out to sea.

I climbed aboard one of the abandoned vessels. In spite of the terrors of the journey two years ago, I loved these boats.

As I watched some young children playing amidst the trash that bobbed among them, I almost forgot about Vu, who was watching me from the beach.

"I see he's following you again," someone said. It was Thang. "Be careful, Tra. He's a bitter man. He blames your father for what happened to his son."

"But why does he follow me all the time?" I asked, glancing at Vu as he stood taut and silent on the beach.

"Beats me," said Thang. "He's dangerous, though. He's fallen in with a crowd of ex-army types. You know, South Vietnamese army. They've been involved in gang battles in the camps."

"We're getting out," I told him by way of changing the subject. "Just in time, too. They say the Western governments don't want any more refugees. Father thinks they might start sending us all back."

"Yes, I heard you'd be going soon. Good luck to you. I just wish it was my turn."

"You'll get word any time now," I said. "I'm sure you will."

Thang smiled, then observed, "Vu's gone. I'll see you, Tra. I've fixed up a card game." Thang began to swing back along the beach on his crutches.

A little way along, he turned and said in a low voice, "Keep an eye on Vu. If he's heard about you leaving...."

"Go on," I said. "Finish what you've got to say."

"No, forget it," said Thang. With that, he headed toward the warehouse.

I began to move from boat to boat, climbing out of one and onto the next. I cast my mind back to the journey. I remembered Hoan's shocked face when that policeman had pushed him aside. I shook my head. Freedom! If there was any freedom for people like us, we'd have to make it ourselves.

I was alone now that Thang and Vu had gone. The playing children were way down the beach. I gazed across the sea. What would Canada be like? Better than here, that was certain. Life was about to begin again. It had never been my choice to leave home, but I now wanted to make our new life work. It would be an insult to Grandmother not to, and an insult to the parents of my adopted sister, Phuong. The brisk wind stung my cheeks. I could smell the sea.

Yes, I really was going to make it work.

"So, you're leaving, are you?"

I spun around at the sound of Vu's harsh, thin voice. His eyes, those blazing eyes, were fixed upon my face.

"What do you want?" I said. My voice was shaky.

"Want? I don't want anything," said Vu.

I tried to step down from the prow of the boat, but Vu stood below me on the beach and blocked my path.

"I don't want anything anymore," he repeated. Something in his voice made me uneasy. It was then that I noticed a long, thin blade sticking out from his sleeve. He had a knife.

"You stop wanting anything from life when they take your son away," said Vu. "The VC killed my boy, you know—your father's VC. But your father's going off to enjoy a comfortable life in Canada, isn't he?"

"He isn't VC," I protested. "He isn't anything anymore. He wants to start over."

"That's right," said Vu with heavy sarcasm. "He wants to start again. That's fine, isn't it? First you destroy a country, then you run away."

I decided to make a run for it. I began to stumble from boat to boat in an attempt to escape.

"It's no use, I've got you now," said Vu. "I've dreamed about this moment."

As I made my way awkwardly along the row

of boats, Vu found it easy to stride along the beach to keep pace with me and deny me an escape route.

"What do you want?" I cried.

"That's simple," said Vu. "Your father took my son from me. Now I'm going to take his from him."

He drew his knife, the long blade glinting in the sunlight. I jumped down into the water between the rotting hulls. Vu advanced, slowly raising his knife. He lunged at me, once, twice, three times. I shrank back. The third time Vu struck, the blade sliced through my shirt near my stomach. A trace of blood seeped onto the cotton. The sight of it drove me to resist. I grabbed the steering pole of the nearest boat and swung it at him. He ducked and came on.

"An eye for an eye," he said coldly, deliberately turning the knife handle in his palm.

As I turned to run, I slipped and fell heavily into the surf.

I struggled to rise, then fell back. I looked up to see Vu standing over me. I clutched at the arm that held the knife, digging my nails into the soft flesh of his forearm. Shrugging my arm off, Vu reached down and gripped my shirt collar. He began to press the knife closer. I renewed my desperate clawing at his arms. I was struggling wildly, but he was far stronger than I.

"Please," I cried. "Don't!"

I pushed wildly at Vu's arms and chest, trying to force him off me. He wasn't going to be stopped by a mere boy. He shoved me down into the waves.

"I haven't done anything to you," I cried, tears blurring my vision. "Why are you doing this?"

Vu wrenched my flailing arms away and hit me across the mouth, numbing my right cheek.

"You're your father's son," he screamed. "That's why I have to do this."

Your father's son! Suddenly that meant something to me. It assumed enormous significance. Grandmother had said it to me once.

I began to fight for my life by tearing at Vu's shirt and kicking at his legs. He was trying to hold me down in the rubbish-filled water, but he was stumbling, swaying. I stared into Vu's face. He was sweating with the effort of subduing me. I felt an immense surge of energy. My father had fought for what he believed in, and now it was my turn to fight for freedom. I wanted to live more than he wanted to kill me. I was going to live. I refused to let everything end here, amid the ruined boats and the trash. Vu looked puzzled and shocked at my renewed resistance.

"You can't do it," I cried, staring into his face. It was true. Maybe if I had given in easily, he could have, but I was fighting for my life. I refused to give it up.

Suddenly something swung behind Vu's head

and clubbed him. He dropped heavily to his knees, then fell face forward. As he fell, I saw Thang brandishing one of his crutches. He dragged Vu out of the water and looked down at the semi-conscious man.

"My debt to your family is repaid," Thang said.

"How did you know we were here?" I asked.

"I just knew," said Thang. "Something told me to come back. I dread to think what would have happened if I hadn't."

Thang leaned over Vu as he stirred. "Go on, Tra, get back to your family. I'll take him back to his wife."

I stared at my attacker. As Vu regained his senses, he began to sob. His whole body was shaking.

"Don't blame him," Thang said to me. "That war did terrible things to people. He's a victim like we all are—a victim, that's all...."

I began to walk quickly toward our living quarters. As I crossed the sand, I could see the guards at the camp gates and the barbed wire. In a few weeks, maybe even days, I would leave all this behind. Beyond the camp, steamy clouds swirled thickly around the upper slopes of the wooded hills.

My pace quickened. I couldn't see the fences or the guards any more, just the hills, the clouds, the sky. I glimpsed Mother and Father hurrying toward me. They looked at once anxious and relieved. I began to run faster and faster. I felt like yelling for sheer joy. No matter what it took, I was going to have this thing called freedom.